THE VAMPIRE BELLE

CHELSEA GAITHER

ACKNOWLEDGMENTS

A big thanks to Vanessa and the other sensitivity readers at Salt and Sage Books. Anything I've gotten right is because of them. Any errors are exclusively my own.

"I hate kids shows about racism," Peter Jennings said. He was my work partner here at Terrestrial Affairs, and currently sported the costume of Ichabod Crane. His vibrantly red hair—a little darker than Celtic ginger—was nearly waist length and, for once, tied down into something approximating the 1700's curls and ponytail, sans pomade. He was Black and very dark skinned, so strangers often figured the ginger came out of a bottle. It didn't. This assumption annoyed him almost as much as the tradition that a Black man with red hair is some kind of sorcerer. Mentioning *that* was a good way to get him to burst into flames. He'd chosen Ichabod for Halloween because someone had once compared him to the literary coward, and he dealt with insults by making them a game. He'd been balancing a Styrofoam pumpkin with artificial flames on his knee all night. He wasn't in a very good mood.

I steered our government-issue navy blue sedan down Ocean Drive in Corpus Christi, Texas, at two AM, heading towards Louisiana Avenue. This is the ritzy, slinky neighborhood in Corpus, a kind of low-rent River Oaks. Still a bit high-end for our normal clients. Movies want you to believe that being a witch, wizard, vampire or similar flavor thereof is a one-way ticket to wealth and celebrity, but truth is, the boogeyman works minimum wage same as the rest of us. It's one reason Terrestrial Affairs exists. Predators target the vulnerable, and the magical are uniquely exposed. Sure, magic means power, but power always comes with new vulnerabilities. Statistically, having magic shortens your lifespan by half, and *that* assumes that you are still human and living.

But the client tonight was in a category all of her own. And she was always a headache.

Normally Pete and I work day shift, but the November Child Annual Rabies push meant all hands on deck at night. The streets this late were mostly deserted. Corpus did have a club scene to attract night fauna, but most of the stragglers kept to downtown, congregating around Doc Rocket's or the Hidden Door. November Child Day is always the first of November, and we are encouraged to head out in costume. Public Relations says it makes our image less scary. Peter's burning pumpkin was an office-wide hit every year. I'd had less luck with the rags and patches of Pippi Longstocking. Our conversation about ignorance of the classics and the merits of kids movies had now brought me to unfamiliar territory.

"Alright, I'll bite. Why do you hate kids shows about racism?" I said.

"Because they let you pretend you've done something. Using a metaphor like, I dunno, kitty cats vs. discount Shirley Temple. What was that movie? Cats can't sing? A metaphor for racism where everything's fixed with a song?"

"Something like that," I said.

"Yeah. But the real problem's still baked into the premise. We get that you see us as a different species. That doesn't need any more reinforcement. You *should* be comparing apples to apples, and you're doing people and felines. And the story is about the cats having to prove they're equal. Having to earn it. You start off saying they're not the same."

I was white. Basically Wonderbread. I considered myself smart on the uptake but this was one area that didn't feel intuitive for me. Pete was on his last nerve, and had been since we got the client list. He was venting. "Or like that kid's movie about a bunny rabbit saving predators in a zoo world? Which was sort of saying that the people discriminated against *are* the predators?" I said.

"Oh, you caught that one?" He said, then nodded. "Yeah. That."

I flipped on my blinker to change lanes again. I'll admit, I was more than a little worried. When we left HQ the first thing Pete had done was shut off his jazz playlist and chunk the phone in the glovebox. At home he went straight for Usher, Beyonce and the Weekend, but he *did* have to behave himself in an Agency car. A typical work-day was an enjoyable soak in classics like Louie Armstrong or BB King. Maybe even Scatman Crothers. The silence was telling. Music was a part of Happy Pete, and Happy Pete hadn't come to work today.

Terrestrial Affairs has jurisdiction over supernatural residents of this plane of existence. We take on supernatural events that involve extradimensional entities and provide specialized investigation services for mundane law enforcement. That's the government copy, anyway. In reality? Supernatural social workers with guns. We soothe ghosts and network them to the *good* exorcists. Same with the legitimately possessed. Werewolves and vampires have their rabies shots updated, and we try to keep the freshly changed away from the gangs and nastier packs. We combat child-targeted Fae propaganda like Tinkerbell, and make sure the Halloween novelty witch kits can't summon anything bigger than the nearest consenting poltergeist. You've got the right to be a witch, a vampire or a were-wolf, but your neighbors also have the right to be safe. Balancing that friction is the heart of what we do.

The workload is hell. Being able to call myself "Agent Astrid Stone" on a business card feels spiffy, but most of the job was just connecting Client A with Resource B, and then doing the paperwork, which is the real monster walking among us. Everything we do has to be accounted for, documented and then billed to the applicable authority. Poltergeist activity got a lot less scary once I understood the ghost just needed cognitive behavioral therapy, but I'm still terrified of the checkboxes on that specific billing sheet.

November Child Day is always November 1st. It memorializes the death of the unidentified Patient Zero in the catastrophic rabies outbreak of 1961. That outbreak, and the political fallout that followed, motivated the government mandate that eventually evolved into Terrestrial Affairs. Every November 1st, educational materials are presented, children escape school, and we go door to door to our at-risk clients and make sure their rabies paperwork is in order.

And as most of those clients are vampires…night shift. My dashboard clock read 2:05 am, and the streetlights raced us by.

"That movie about aliens in South Africa was pretty decent," I said.

Peter rubbed his temple. "They were portraying apartheid with *literal aliens*. That's as other-species as you can get. And the ones that really grind my gears are the ones that use vampirism as a metaphor. Like that HBO show with the pretty blond chick. Vampires suffer from discrimination!" He let that statement drip sarcasm on the dashboard for a few seconds, then added, "And hey, here's a good idea. Let's showcase that in the *south*." He shook his head, laughing silently to himself.

"Not to be the devil's advocate, but they kind of do," I said. Sure, vampires got grandfathered into the Rights of Magical Persons Act in 1969 but it wasn't a felony to kill one without a warrant until the late 80s. And if they wanted to qualify for most social aid, they had to have current rabies shots, hence our outing tonight. It was more than a little dehumanizing to get the same shots as the family dog if you wanted to avoid life-shattering fines.

Peter gave me one of his patented, blister-chrome-off-a-trailer-hitch *looks*. "Astrid. What's the demographic breakdown on American vampires again? The ones over fifty? The kind they make movies about?"

Right.

Vampires skew white. *Really* white. If I am Wonderbread, they're dissolved in bleach. There are arguments about random selection and chance, but that's just window dressing. Vampires skew white because the vampire Masters—the older, magical powerhouses who typically lead gangs—are mostly White Anglo-Saxon Protestants who only ever turn other WASPs, and the Masters are typically the best at keeping their fledglings alive. The majority of over-fifties in the south that weren't a Master's pet survived under the sheets of a certain group with a fondness for, let's say, a real specific trio of *konsonants*.

That part doesn't make it into the movies much.

When Terrestrial Affairs was formed via the RMPA, thus giving future me a job, the undead from other races began living long enough to see a couple anniversaries and maybe sire their own fledglings. Attitudes in the undead community began to change. But new vampires don't typically last long. The average lifespan for a vampire is six months from date of turning. And that average *includes* the multi-century old survivors like Dracula. The new recruits we lovingly call the Fluffy Intern Pool come fresh out of college with visions of wooden stakes, garlic, and holy water. A lot of them leave once they understand the mandate is to keep vampires alive. Which is harder than it looks. All agents of Terrestrial Affairs know a dead vampire. It's a good week if you aren't flushing ash off your work shoes. Under the RMPA, vampires *do* have a right to exist. And if a vampire's specific attitude chafed at you, you practiced tolerance or found another job.

Normally, Peter was the example to follow. Tonight? Not so much.

There was a small chance this was romantic tension. I'd seen him wound this tight before, typically when he got dumped by whatever narcissistic pretty boy he'd brought home. Not that my own romantic life was any better. He and I had nearly identical taste in asshole exs. We'd bonded over drunk, ugly crying sessions and self-help tomes with titles like *"Why Does He Do That"*. The only major difference is that I'd had one big ex, and bailed on new men if they even smelled like the same bad aftershave. Peter kept trying to make pretty work. I recognized Peter's dour expression from the romantic discard phase. But usually he'd have something of a honeymoon before the new pretty's mask slipped.

No. I knew the client was the problem. The rant about racism was the clencher.

"At least nobody mistook you for the queen of childhood overcompensation," I said, as we parked on Louisiana. I *liked* Pippi Longstocking. Everyone had called me Pollyanna.

"It's because you're white and optimistic and that movie was on the Hallmark channel last night," Peter said, glowering, as we got out of the car.

"I had red yarn braids held up by wire," I said. I'd ditched the wig when we grabbed our case files and put on the Moon Silver jewelry our boss makes us wear. Moon Silver is bank-breaking expensive, but Dark Fae, vampires and Inducted members of Deep Cults are all allergic to the stuff. Plus it's the only metal that can hold a vampire's reflection. When your job description includes servicing all but the latter, it's a rather good idea to make it a regular fashion choice.

"Yeah. I saw them. You're lucky they're not calling you Raggedy Ann," Peter said, then glared up at the current client's house. "Fine. Let's get Camille over with."

Older vampires understand that as far as fashion accessories go, a good image and loyal patrons are a must for survival. Camille Ward had spent decades cultivating the cotillion and debutante crowd. She presented as one part Scarlett O'Hara, two parts Steel Magnolias. A shining survivor of the Antebellum South and a homing missile aimed right at the country clubs set, where Southern Nostalgia is its own genre. Of course, the persona might have suffered somewhat if the RMPA pardons hadn't gotten her records sealed. Some centenarian vamps survived quite nicely without wanton murder orgies. Camille hadn't been one of them.

Dealing with her always wound Pete up.

Part of it was the local attitude. Any other vampire with her track record would have been immediately considered a problem child, but half the office seemed in love with her. The other agents seemed indifferent, if a little too willing to let her notoriety rub off on them. I was in Pete's minority; something about her stroked me the wrong way. Camille had moved to Texas by way of New Orleans when tornadic storms decimated her historic former plantation in Kentucky. She shifted from Houston to Corpus because Houston's Master Vampire despised her. She was already here when Peter and I began working together six years ago. Each November, we trotted up to her door and endured the theatrical sighs and occasional angry rant about how she was not a (pardon her language) damn dog, she didn't need a (pardon her language) damn dog tag and bless her heart (flutter of fingers and eyelids, extra honey on that pure Georgia Peach accent) if this wasn't more than she could stand. Cue fanning motion as if it were possible for her to feel hot.

This was always followed by an attempt to get Peter to come inside and eat something. Vampires can't eat, by the way. Anything edible would have been catered for our benefit. Each year we left, feeling dirty. And each year Peter took a detour to the magnolia tree growing at the corner of Camille's spacious home and shit into her begonia bed.

The first couple times he did it, I told him it was stupid and he *would* be fired. That was when he told me Camille had refused to work with any other agent. He *wanted* her to make a complaint, but so far it hadn't happened. Camille was going to be his client, or Camille wasn't going to be *anybody's* client. And our Director, who had all the bedside manner of dry ice, had told Peter to suck it up.

We walked up to her door, and Peter was already eyeing that magnolia. "Huh. She replanted. It's a zinnia bed now."

"Pokier leaves. I'm more curious about how that thing is *always* blooming." I said.

"She pays a Fae landscaping company to do it. If it doesn't freeze too bad, the tree survives." Then, while he loosened his costume's ascot, "You know, I *could* do this alone. You can go do Sanctuary House." The halfway house on the south side of town was for newbie vamps; there were always five or six fledglings in residence. Some of them even lived long enough to graduate.

But Camille wanted Peter.

"Hey, I got your back, sport," I said. "You're not leaving me behind."

"You keep calling me sport, I'm gonna gag you and lock you in the trunk next to the emergency kit." He said.

I grinned at him. "You promise?"

He threw his ascot at me.

Camille's house was a replica of a French Quarter apartment block. Red brick, wrought iron painted green on the upper floor balconies. It stood out, even on this street. This was not Camille's creation. It predated her arrival by a couple decades. Almost as if it were meant to be…or so she said every time we interviewed her.

I knocked on her door.

Or at least, I tried to.

I had expected the resistance of a latched door, but it creaked opened at my touch. "Camille?" I called out and eased in, only to stumble over a spread of fabric draped carelessly in the foyer. The hallway within was illuminated by a set of crystal-and-brass imitation gas lamps. They gave the black and white patterned tile a dreamy quality and glimmered in the pile of crumpled silk and crinolines sitting on the floor, topped by a wagon-wheel hat festooned with damaged feathers. The scent of gun smoke almost overpowered the remnant of decay. But I couldn't mistake that smell. Not when the ash swirling out of Camille's clothes left those neat, white stains where it settled on my shoes.

All agents of Terrestrial Affairs know a dead vampire.

Chapter Two

"Any clue on the cause of death?" I asked. The vampire vac almost drowned me out. I'm pretty sure it had a more dignified name; mortuary branding is all about an atmosphere of respect. The thing was still a black, glorified dust buster with silvery pinstripes like some kind of race car. It had a triple-deluxe industrial grade HEPA filter that should be able to make its own coffee, but it needed to be top grade. Vampire ash is some of the finest particulate known to man. The forensic witch hit the red "stop" button and glared at me. Magdalena turned "not in a good mood" into a weapon somewhat akin to a howitzer. Not that I blamed her. A dead vampire meant we had to call in both the cops and our own forensic department. Our people got there first. As usual, mundane law enforcement didn't want to touch this crime scene. They arrived, noted vampire ash, and departed more rapidly than Camille would have upon running into a Catholic priest. Assuming she'd been Catholic, of course.

Terrestrial Affairs' mandate is technically more social work than law enforcement, but the reality is that mundane cops aren't equipped to handle supernatural-related crime, especially when the paranormal creature is the victim. That is, by the way, the official term. If you are not magical, you are mundane. It says nothing about your professionalism, although there were some badges who fit that descriptor comprehensively. And even the best mundane forensic training cannot cover the knowledge base of an occult expert, any more than someone with a Ph.D. in occult studies can interpret blood splatter reliably. This was part of what made TA's forensic personnel so special. They are trained in both disciplines and require the doctorates, plural, to prove it.

Which brought me to Maggie. AKA Magdalena Gonzales, the top occult expert and top forensic specialist south of Victoria. Her specialties were syncretic religion, Latinx witchery, and fiber analysis. She used science as her primary weapon—it was more admissible in court, and much less scary—and could spackle the gaps with magic faster than you could say "exoneration". She'd clawed her way to the top of a formidable pile, and it showed. The cops gave her both respect and space. Even tonight, when Maggie was painted up like a Dios de la Muertos sugar skull, they treated her with the significant deference they neglected with the rest of us. The only difference between her face paint and her usual layer of makeup was color and consistency. She applied her foundation with all the enthusiasm of van Gogh with a palette knife and her patron saints appeared to be MAC and Sephora. She identified as Latinx first, Catholic second, Witch third. You were welcome to argue with her on how appropriate or valid her choices were. She'd make you into intellectual hash, then help you pick up the pieces. She was what she was, and you accept it or get out of her crime scene.

Maggie smiled at me, sweetly, with lips painted to look like teeth. "Camille Ward, cause of death: Consumption, March 18th, 1862," She said, and revved the vampire vac. "Only to rise again two days later and become our problem."

"Ha. Ha. Ha. *Ha.*" Peter said. And glared at her.

She sighed and held up a small plastic bag with a slightly deformed slug in it. "Looks like a nine mil. Decent gun. Glock, maybe a Sig."

"Silver?" I asked. Yahoos going after supernaturals assume that silver bullets work on things that aren't werewolves.

"Normal lead, which means they hit her heart," Maggie said.

"You can tell that from a bullet?" I said.

She flipped into teach-mode. "A vampire is a corpse animated by magic. That power moves through the vascular system as a pathway, with the heart as a hub. Disrupt that, and the vampire's dead. Er. More dead. It doesn't matter what you use. I knew one person who killed a vampire with a fiberglass reflector off the end of a driveway. Bullet through the heart, the magic's done. There's a matching bullet hole in her corset. I'm scanning the ashes for any trace magic, but all I can sense are the leftovers from vampires dying."

"That leaves an aura?" I said.

"Same way an explosion leaves smoke. What a way to go. Nearly a hundred fifty years old, and it's a bullet that gets her. Well, it could be worse." She paused. Glanced at Peter. "Brace yourself on the press coverage for this one. Somebody is already dialing up all the news desks. They're calling her a 'national treasure' on Twitter."

Peter went still. "Excuse me?" He said.

Her expression softened. "That's what I heard. The death of the Last Great Southern Belle." Maggie sucked up a little pile of white particulate that had gathered around a vase. She and Peter shared a look between them, the sort that always seemed to eclipse me. I would have called it *excluded*, but it felt more like a shadow cast across a barren path. I was the path. "You'd think that the vampire thing would put a damper on all this enthusiasm. Scarlet O'Hara she was not," Maggie said.

"She wasn't even Melanie Wilkes," Peter said. "Where's the remains going to go?"

"About three different historical societies will fight over her. They're not too hot on the undead angle but she is a part of history. She has no surviving family, so when they find out she doesn't have a will, because *of course* old fangs never do, it's gonna go to probate. She's going to wind up in a museum. Maybe the one occupying her old plantation." She set the dust buster down. "You okay, mijo?"

Peter sighed and rubbed his eyes. He looked so tired. "Sure we can't put her in a cat box?"

"Pete," Maggie said, and most of the gentleness left her tone. "I know, okay? I get it. But she's a client. This has to be played by the book."

"It never matters, does it?" He said, words drifting feather soft to the ashy tile at his feet. It did matter to Pete, though. His eyes burned with unspoken feeling. When you work with somebody long enough, you feel their upset, like the first vibrations in their private earthquake country. These were the flashing lights before an 8.5 shaker.

"The house across the street had cameras," I said, quickly. "Maybe we should go take a look."

"Yeah," Peter said. "Do our job right." But he glared at the beetle-black dust buster one more time before we left the room.

"Camille loved Halloween."

The neighbor with the cameras loved Camille. She greeted us, all dolled up as Marilyn Monroe. Her name made less of an impact than her wig of peroxide curls. As she said those words, *loved Halloween,* her pale face flushed as with excitement or arousal, and her hands fluttered theatrically. She kept glancing at the growing number of cars lining Louisiana Avenue like an aging Bette Davis searching for an audience. There are some women who age gracefully, like cathedrals. I had the sense that this lady could have been one of them, if she'd left herself to time. But she had tightened her skin like a drumhead, and the few lines remaining were haunted by the ghosts of smiles that never existed.

Her house reminded me of a *Southern Life* magazine if you tore out the decorating pages and layered them one over another. Themed hoarding. Rustic, worn wood furniture, including end-tables with imaginary ranch brands on them. Cowhide rug. Decorative plates and strategic deployment of autumn-leaf topiaries. Antiques that would have been tasteless if they were a decade younger, but that now qualified as "character" because they cost more. She even had a couple red-lipped, black-faced china children strategically hidden behind a large, glitter-studded pumpkin.

"She was over here all the time you know. Over here just last night. She'd found the best canape tray, she just begged me to try it. I couldn't believe it when she moved in. I'd grown up with Tara and Rhett and Viviane Leigh, and to have a *real live Southern Belle* on our street? It was almost…the dream." She sighed and turned her head away, I think to hide the thrilled little smile playing at the edge of her lips.

"Can we go back and see your cameras, ma'am?" Peter said.

There was a brief, angry flush on her cheeks, but she nodded. With quick, sharp motions, she took me by the arm and whisked me towards the back of her house. I looked back at Peter in desperation. *Save me.* He left me to languish in her cloud of Opium perfume, trailing behind with a strained grin.

"And Halloween, oh, Halloween is just…*special,*" Marilyn said. "She always dresses like she did back in the good days. She has the loveliest collection of antique dresses. You might even fit in a couple of the bigger ones, honey, if she corseted you up good." Marilyn squeezed my shoulders. I swallowed the insult and my response. A reply wasn't worth my time. "Last year we invited her to *Las Donas* and she came in period perfect dress. I wanted us to do a *Gone with the Wind* theme one year. The first year she arrived. But they wouldn't let us do that."

Las Donas de la Corte was the annual scholarship event tied to the Buccaneer Days Parade. Corpus's version of debutants get elected to a court as Queen, Princess and a dozen odd Duchesses, all in elaborate fancy dress. They get scholarships. The clothes are the real stars of the show, enormous monstrosities with ten-foot-long trains and a metric ton of crystals and sequins. Each year they have a "theme," which is sometimes well-thought, and sometimes…not so much.

"*They* wouldn't let us," Marilyn repeated, and glanced once at Peter. Her grip on my arm tightened. I felt like I was being frog-marched by a perfume bottle past the walls of kitsch aged into an antique respectability. "Your costume is *darling.* I did love Pollyanna as a child. I always try to be like her. Hopefulness that can save a community. We do so need to look more *forward* in the world. To be more *positive.* In a world of such darkness and negativity, A little kindness paid forward would change everything. Here we are. The camera closet. Paid forward. Wasn't that another movie?"

I dislike *Pollyanna* for *reasons.* My mother, who I never talk to, had her own form of Pollyanna's positivity. She called it Keeping Sweet. Title, caps required and some underlines for emphasis. Everything in my childhood revolved around Keeping Sweet with a rigid grace that always felt like it was one tremble away from shattering. The first time I read about *parentification* it was like reading a roadmap of my own childhood. But at least I'd only been exploited by my parents. Pollyanna had been parentified by an entire damn town. I reacted to her camera closet like a drowning human to a ladder. Anything to escape asphyxiation by *Opium.*

Marilyn's security cameras, naturally, were the cheapest things on the market. As a positive, though, they recorded to digital and there was something to work with.

"Do you think we should call the cops in before we review anything?" I asked Peter.

His jaw was so tight I was worried for his teeth. "Let's just…let's just see it. Just let me see it."

I was suddenly glad Marilyn wasn't paying attention to Peter. I brought up the recording for the night and backed it up to a flash drive—always keep flash drives in your pockets—before I began our playback.

Vampires can be active during the day. They burn in direct sunlight but can endure indirect with moderate discomfort. Houses with big, shady lawns and blacked out windows are thus favorites among the fanged populace. Camille was on the south side of Louisiana, facing north, and there were several large live oaks in her yard beside Peter's favorite magnolia. With the sun setting in the south-west, she would have had enough shade to risk opening her front door at five. Start the recording there, as fast as it will go. Play.

The first set of trick-or-treaters, adorable in costume and themed masks, began skipping up the sidewalk at nearly six pm. With fast-forward enabled, they looked like Santa's tiny elves on crack. The intermittent herds of children went up to Camille's door, which opened and revealed something that looked like a slightly pixelated, frothy, exploded cupcake. I assumed that was Camille in crinolines. You couldn't see her face, but even from across the street you could make out her cleavage. The trick or treaters dithered around at the front door for a bit, then sped down the walk at hyper speed.

Six p.m. became seven. Seven became eight. Nine o'clock, and the flood of adorable polyester costumes had shrunk to a small trickle, the children coming now in ones or twos. At 9:45, a singular pair walked up to the house. One adult. One child. The door opened, motions were made…and the frothy cupcake vanished behind a closing door as the pair raced off into the night.

"That's it," Peter and I said at the same time. I scrambled for the playback controls.

I reset the recording to 9:40, set to normal speed. Play.

The last person to see Camille in her un-life was a tall white woman in dark-colored scrubs, indeterminate on the black and white recording, and a very small child dressed like a cowboy. I couldn't get a good view of the kid around their cowboy hat. She carried the child. Her movements dragged a little bit before she finally set the kid down. This late, a kid that small would be exhausted. Barring growth restrictions, the kid couldn't have been over five.

Camille opened the door before they even had a chance to knock. There was no sound and no color. They were too far away to even guess what was said. Camille began making dramatic gestures, fanning herself, fluttering her hands like a showboat ferry gone full-steam. As I watched the interaction, I white-knuckled my USB pen. And not out of concern for the soon-to-be-dead-undead. Making eye contact with an older vampire like Camille is never a bright idea. After a certain age, vampires exercise a form of mind control. It doesn't blank out the will of the target, just overrides the mind's control of the body. It takes eye contact to start the process. The term we use these days is "rolling" or "rolling under". This control is broken when the vampire either loses interest or dies. Camille was in Maggie's dust buster so this sick feeling in my gut was moot, but it still sat uneasy.

The adults talked for a moment, then Mom set the kid down and they took up a gunslinger stance. Camille clapped her hands, then gestured between mother and child. The mother nodded. Camille closed her front door slightly, vanishing from sight for a couple heartbeats.

"It looks like she's reaching for something," Peter said.

"Maybe a present? She loves giving presents," Marilyn said, beaming.

Camille reappeared and knelt in front of the child. It took about thirty seconds for her to then stand and nod to the mother. No one was watching the child, who struggled to grip whatever they'd been handed.

Peter and I shared a look. He didn't need to ask me. I restarted the recording again, this time at 9:45, when they turned up the walk. The kid had something similar to Camille's gift already, and they pointed it at her when she put her hands up, *you got me, sheriff.* When she handed her gift over, the kid suddenly couldn't keep his hands up. She'd given him something heavy. In fact...

"She gave the kid a gun," I said.

"She's not that stupid," Peter disagreed.

We went over it again. And again. And each time, it seemed more and more clear: Camille handed a five-year-old, if that, a gun.

We kept watching. Once more, Camille held up her hands as if being arrested, *you got me, sheriff.* Then there was a flash. Camille stood frozen, her hands to her breast, and then a cloud formed as her clothes collapsed around her dissolving body. And once more, the concealing door swung closed.

The presumed mother slapped something from her kid's hands, looked around, picked up her child and ran.

Peter said, "What the hell?"

"The kid shot her," I said.

"She always gave the little Black kids extra," Marilyn said, and sighed. Her eyes glimmered wetly. One hand went to her breastbone. "A true class act. A *real* Southern Belle. It would be horrible if one of the little pic…" A pause. A glance at Peter. "It would be a shame. Killed by what she loved so much." Pause for emphasis. "Halloween."

Mr. DeMille, I'm ready for my closeup. I thought. Had discount Marilyn here ever had a dead guy floating in her pool?

Peter rewound to the moment Camille's cloud-like dress went poof. The woman again slapped an object from her child's hands before she grabbed him up and ran.

"Pete. We need to get this to the cops. It's not our job past this."

He watched it a couple times more. "Yeah. I just…That's a *baby,* almost. Who would give a *baby* a *gun*?"

"You never know with some children," Marilyn said. "It's those video games. They make everyone violent." She shook her head, letting both fake blond curls and real ones shadow her face for a moment. Neither of us said anything. "She was from another time, you understand. They didn't have all this confusion about guns and…and…and back then they *valued* their Second Amendment rights." She patted me on the shoulder. "You know? Train them up early. That would have been her motto, back in the day." And her eyes got dreamy. She pulled a cigarette out of her pack, lit it, and blew a cloud of nicotine vaguely in Peter's direction. "Such a shame," She said. "The type of people we let into our neighborhoods."

I didn't know I had moved forward until Peter caught me. "Yeah," he said, tightening his grip on my arm, and meeting her sub-zero gaze. His seemed almost to burn. "It's a real damn shame, the kind of people here."

Chapter Three

The police watched the security clip five times, then told us that they were taking jurisdiction. Now that the prime suspect was still sleeping in pull ups, they were all over it. It was just the way things worked. Terrestrial Affairs agents weren't cops. Maggie would keep us in the loop. It was now about 4:30 am, we had to finish our client list and the paperwork before we could go home. All of these were good reasons to let it go.

Still, Peter pulled Maggie aside. "You make *sure* that they use the word accident. It looks like it was her gun."

"Definitely was her gun. Damn thing so soaked with vampire magic you'd think it was about to ask for a cup of o negative," Maggie said. "It's not our jurisdiction anymore, but I'll try."

"Don't try, Mags. Do it." He checked himself. Took a deep breath. "The neighbor seemed pretty sure that this kid was Black."

"Was he?" She looked from him to me and back.

"Between his hat and the distance, we never got a good enough look," I said.

"Peter." Maggie's voice was soft, steel in a velvet glove. "Mijo. All I can do is try."

He nodded, lips pursed, jaw clenched tight. I kept expecting to hear his bones break under the anxious clench of his body. "When they find him…" He trailed off. Closed his eyes, and his whole body shuddered. "I just hope the peroxide blonde up there is racist instead of right," He said.

Maggie sighed, patted his hand. "Peter. It *will* be okay." She said.

I just wish it had sounded more reassuring.

The rest of the client list took us past dawn. Most of the living dead were compliant. One of them also ranted about "checking dog tags". He got our referral for an extra therapy appointment. On the drive back from Sanctuary House, I flipped the radio to the hard rock morning show and frowned. They were talking about Camille.

This was why I hated November Child Day. It ended with dead vampires. Sanctuary House had been its usual depressing bust. Of the ten names we'd been given when we compiled our client list last week, only four were still ambulatory. Two were little piles of ash with no explanation, one was in the long, slow process of dying because he'd eaten a hamburger, and three were completely MIA. And while Camille's Second Death was a surprise, I kept thinking about the guy who ate the hamburger. It hadn't even been a good burger. McDonalds, off the dollar menu, and dry. As if the ketchup, mustard and special sauce were any more lethal.

This was why vampires were high priority clients. Master Vampires and centenarians like Camille commercialize their image of power and glory. But for every Master, there's a couple hundred hamburger guys. They're people. Sad, lonely, desperate people who are only a few months removed from the end of everything they ever knew. Hamburger Guy hadn't bought the thing to eat. Just to… taste it. Get the feeling of eating again. Then he could pretend for five seconds that he still needed to breathe, that he could feel sunlight again. That his old life was waiting like an empty suit on a changing table, and he could just put it on and go home. And then muscle memory took over and he swallowed. Game over.

That's why I work TA. Not to deal with things like Camille, but to talk down the Hamburger Guys. I could have at least given him less-lethal alternatives. It hadn't been about the food; it had been about feeling human again for just a few seconds.

And Vampires fear death. Every vampire's account of their turning contains a moment when they are offered a choice. They can have their unlife or they can have *something else*. Most religions have tried to claim that this *something else* is evidence for God and an afterlife, but the literature doesn't agree on what this thing is, just that the choice is there. Every vampire, all of them, straight across the board, regret choosing unlife.

People justify killing Vampires with the theory that the Second Death brings them back to God. The original Hunter Lodges even got a papal dispensation for it. A vampire can even, apparently, choose to die on their own. They have some grand moment of ideological apotheosis and turn into ash on the spot. But the vast majority of them want to *live*, and settle for un-life. It isn't fair, or right, to take that away from them, any more than it'd be right to take my life away from me. And it made me angry when the bad actors got all the attention.

Like the morning show.

Someone had really gotten their teeth into Camille's death. It sounded like they were whipping social media up into a frenzy. Apparently, there'd been a deluge of photographs and video clips sent to every news desk in the country. Those pretty doe-eyed, blond headshots might as well have been catnip. The morning show guys wouldn't shut up about her. And her being a vampire just added to the mystique.

"Why is everybody going nuts over this?" I said, while changing lanes quick. "The woman never accomplished anything." Driving though morning traffic made me irritable when I *did* get enough sleep the night before.

Peter said nothing for a few moments. He was already working through the small hill of paperwork we had to finish before we could go home. We had to stop by the police station to report our missing Sanctuary clients *as* missing. The odds were they were dead too, but we couldn't make that assumption without filing missing persons reports. This meant a stop at CCPD.

As we turned into the cops' parking lot, Peter said, "Was that a rhetorical question? About Camille?"

"Well…yeah," I said. Between us the words *National treasure* floated up and drifted away, untethered to reality. "Because she wasn't that. *Nobody* should have treasured that woman."

When the Rights of Magical Persons Act was passed in 1969, vampires got a blanket pardon via one of the bill's uglier compromises. Camille had been one of the beneficiaries. Her most recent documented murder was in 1967. She was an open secret back then, the guest invited to parties to add the spice of anathema to the soiree. In another few years she would become one of Andy Warhol's darlings, then transition back into the upper echelons of polite Southern society as soon as the art scene quit being profitable. That genteel image was still ahead of her when a body was found in the back room of a club.

There was evidence he was a drug user, knowledge that he was a drinker. He had sclerosis of the liver. He was probably being used as a "filter" for vampire parties. Vampires could and *did* safely get high off the blood of drug users, but the "filters" tend to…wear out quick. This guy hadn't been an accidental death, though. He'd been found in four pieces. The blood had been drained, and what hadn't been consumed was left in a single Waterford crystal flute, topped with lemon. In 1970, after the vampire pardons, someone found a photograph of Camille with that glass in her hand, darkness on her lips. When questioned, she admitted to killing him, secure in the knowledge that she would not be prosecuted for it.

That photo became her headshot when she made her cinema debut—all ten minutes of screen time in a biopic about her more famous cousin, Sally. She had it colorized. Red glimmering like rubies from every magazine stand. All of America saw her with her victim's blood garnished like a cocktail. It was obvious to me that Camille hadn't been rehabilitated by the RMPA. She'd been restrained.

Peter was very quiet as we pulled into CCPD HQ's parking lot. Then he said, "I wish you really meant it. That you really wanted to know. Almost as much as I wish you could figure it out on your own."

"Excuse me?" I said.

"Nevermind," He said.

"I'm serious. What did I say wrong?"

"Just…I can't right now, Astrid. Just let it go." And he got out of the car.

Our one cordial ally at CCPD is Matt Baker. He took our reports with a kindly, grandfatherly smile, handed us yet more forms, and took a couple extra minutes to give us a little extra coffee while we checked off boxes.

"Are they looking for the kid? The one that shot Camille Ward?" Peter asked.

"Yeah. We ID'd him and the mother when his dad reported them missing. Kid's name is Joseph Harris. Mom's name is Julia. The dad has no clue where they'd go, but I don't know how far I'd trust that. They got an APB out on their car so this kid can't go far. Dumbest choice in the world to run but I guess they didn't know about the cameras. Nice call on those, by the way."

"He's being charged?" I asked, surprised. He was a *kid*.

"A woman's dead, Stone. Maybe she's a blood sucker, but she still deserves due process." Baker said.

I damn near buried my eyebrows in my hairline, they raised so high. Yes, she *was* that bad. "The woman had a body count, Baker."

He shrugged. I looked to Peter, who appeared to be calculating his words much more carefully than I had mine. "The gun belonged to Ward. She gave the kid the gun, and he could barely hold it," He finally said.

"We have to do the full investigation," Baker said. "It's what's fair and right."

"Right," Peter said, with tone.

"Look…I don't like it either, Jennings. But this is the way the world works. This is what we have to do for us to have a peaceful society. Rule of law *has* to be followed." Baker said.

"How old is this kid?" Peter said.

"Four," Baker said.

"And do I need to ask you what color he is?" Peter said.

"I don't appreciate that hostility," Baker said.

"And I don't appreciate that you plan on arresting a four-year-old Black kid because a hundred-fifty-year-old *plantation owner* couldn't manage proper gun safety."

Baker sighed. He was a very tall, pale white man, like the grandfather I'd never gotten. But suddenly it felt as if he and Peter were on different planets, and I was stuck on some satellite, watching. "Maybe, Jennings," he said, softly, "You're making this out to be something it isn't."

"Am I?" Peter's jaw was approaching can-crushing levels of tension. Baker finally looked away.

"Wrap it up quick, kids. I need to go home," Baker said, and closed the office door.

I couldn't explain why, but my mouth tasted bitter. Nor could I explain why those soft and grandfatherly words from Baker burned. *This is what we have to do.*

I was missing something here. Something important.

I wish you could figure it out on your own.

By the time we got back to HQ, Camille was the running story of the hour. Our breakroom was glass-fronted, and the TV was visible from my cubicle. Her beautiful face, hair the color of golden wheat in perfectly styled curls, was featured every five minutes or so, along with the headline *Manhunt on for killer tot.*

That made me pause. Killer tot? She'd given the kid the gun!

Coffee. I needed coffee. I had enough paperwork to bury bigfoot. I did not *need* to think about the stupid mess Camille had made by dying. I could just leave it behind. Shuck it off like a coat. Maybe that was the best approach.

But even the coffee machine wasn't a refuge. Max Arrows was probably my least favorite intern, ever, and he had a fresh-faced blond student pinned beside the coffee machine. This girl had that *done* look. If there was a betting pool on her internship, whoever had today marked "quit" was about to make a lot of money. I hoped that Max was at least *invited* to ooze all over the kid. I tuned in to the conversation, just to make sure.

"—that black guy, you know? The one they, I don't know, sat on or some shit up north? They made a big deal of him dying in custody, and nobody paying attention. But you get a class act like Camille and she doesn't get half of that focus. She's a victim of a *crime* and people don't care in the least. And it's not *fair--*"

I set the cup down, "Really, Max? You too?"

"Hey, Stone, you explain to me why that lady doesn't deserve all that and more. She was *class*. Look at her." And his eyes turned lovingly to the screen.

Oh, I saw her. I'd seen her in that red velvet dress more than once, in person. She'd gotten the photographs airbrushed so you couldn't see the moles and pores or how she'd never found a foundation that matched bloodless skin. And of course that photo with the cut crystal glass, blood dribbling provocatively out of the corners of her mouth, from her pre-pardon days.

"You ever looked up how many murders there are in her case file?" I said.

"She got the same pardon the rest of them got. We're supposed to treat them like the murders didn't happen." Max said.

And he was right, goddamn it. We *were* supposed to ignore anything that happened before the RMPA. Maybe they were all right. Maybe we *should* be treating this kid—my brain couldn't process that thought. It just felt so obviously wrong.

So I turned to the coffee machine. You *can* make angry coffee. You just have to be careful on your sugar pour. I made mine way too sweet. As I sipped it, I thought, *Put it away, Stone. Just finish your work and go home.*

But I couldn't. I seriously did not *get* this. Camille didn't hide who she was, she just decorated it with velvet and lace. What was I missing?

Coffee in hand, I went to the paperwork office to drop off the missing persons reports. If any of the missing turned up, or anybody connected to them was already in our system, we'd get a red flag within a couple hours. Most of the files never got a ping. Sometimes families hang around after you're turned. Usually, they don't.

My thoughts felt like snags on a sweater. There was something more to this Camille thing, and I felt stuck at surface depth, stuck with the snags. Pull, and the whole thing is ruined. Speak the secret words aloud and watch the whole edifice fall. But did I *really* want to pull this thread? How did I know I'd like what it attached to?

That's when I heard the sound shift. Peter should have been headed to his desk, but I guessed he wanted some coffee too. Now he stood between Max and Dominique Lavell, who in turn was half wrapped around the intern, as if shielding her from both men.

"Back the *fuck up*, Arrows," Peter said, and his fists said more. Something bad was about to go down.

Chapter Four

"What the hell is wrong with you?" Max said. "I was just talking to her."

"Yeah. The way wolves like to just talk to sheep. She already told me about the last time she got paired up with you." Peter's scowl increased moment by moment, as if he were digging it by the shovelful. Yeah, there were a lot of reasons why I did not like Max.

He bristled like an enraged rooster. "You do your own business, Jennings. I got mine handled and last I heard you weren't chasing that kind of tail."

"Neither are you. Anybody who'd worship Camille Ward ought to get an STD panel before they even think about dating." Peter said.

"At least she was class and not some fucking gang-banger reject wannabe F—"

Peter hit him. A full blow, solid, hard on the chin. The sound echoed through the room like a gunshot. And then the rest of us were there, pulling him off of Arrows before it could go much further. I was the one who grabbed his arm. "Pete, stop. Pete. It isn't worth it. Peter, P—ow!"

I spilled my coffee. Hot liquid splashed over us both, soaking into my shirt and both of our pants. It was the touch of heat that broke Peter out of his rage. He blinked, then dropped his fists as if they were on fire. He looked at them for a moment, then at Max, who cupped his reddening jaw and stared at Pete in shock.

"You hit me," He said, surprise in his eyes.

Peter's breath accelerated, as if he'd been running for miles. "Jesus. Oh god. Max. I'm sorry," he said. His voice shook. He sounded like he was about to cry, and he wobbled on his feet in a way that made consciousness an accomplishment. Pete was about to pass out on the floor. I felt cold, and it wasn't from the coffee. This was one hell of an overreaction to punching an idiot who deserved it.

"No. You're not sorry. But you're gonna be." Max said. The short little white man turned around, hand still clasped to his cheek, and marched towards our director's office. He looked like a pissed off duck. A short one.

Peter's eyes were wide, white and wild. "I just killed my career." He said. Quick breaths, like a trapped rabbit. "Oh God, I just…I just almost…God."

Yep. Panic attack. Okay. One step at a time. I assessed the people around me and figured Dominique Lavell was the nearest thing we had to a steady adult. "Get him back to his desk and get him some water."

"I got ya. Been here a few times myself," Domi said, and her *here* encompassed an arena of emotion I was mercifully less used to visiting. She guided him back to his desk gently, whispering to him all the way. She said, "*water*", to the girl Peter had rescued from Max.

Alright. Pete was safe for the moment. Next step: Get Maggie.

Magdalena was a witch. Witchcraft does some incredibly powerful things, but its foundation is the manipulation of emotional energies. This makes them emotional caretakers more often than not, the same way an expert in nuclear power become caretakers for reactors. They don't like having the emotional extremes, and their concurrent explosions of power, if they can help it. If anybody could back Peter off the cliff right now it was going to be Magdalena.

Her office was in the rear of the building, in a soundproof, fireproof area set aside both for her lab and for our evidence holding system. Our independent labs were one of the foundations of the job. It keeps the police from having to touch magical artifacts—and it ensures our clients can't be framed for something that they did not do.

Music is allowed if it bothers no-one. The soundproofing gave Maggie free reign in her domain. I walked into the violins and guitars of the local Tejano station playing *Reggae Kumbia*. Maggie was examining something fine and red under the microscope. She'd replaced her bone-covered costume leotard with a more sensible loose white blouse and black jeans. She looked up. The sugar skull makeup had been replaced with a perfect foundation match, ruby lipstick and winged eyeliner that *almost* hid her exhaustion. "You okay?"

"I am. Pete's not. He's having a panic attack. He just sucker punched Arrows."

Maggie smiled. "Couldn't have happened to a nicer dipshit."

"Well, the dipshit is bitching to the director. Pete thinks he just sunk his career."

Maggie snorted. "Over *Arrows*? Please. The boss isn't going to break one of her golden children over *that*. She's just gonna use it to carve another pound of flesh out of Peter." She rose and crossed the room to the enamel cabinet beneath her Guiana Chestnut. Most people called it a Money Tree plant. Maggie had gotten it from someone she didn't want to offend, but she also didn't practice Feng Shui. She'd taped a piece of paper to make sure everyone understood that in this office, the plant was a Guiana (red sharpie underscore) Chestnut (red sharpie underscore) period. Over her head a large poster of Selena Quintanilla looked down at me with that trademark smile. With quick fingers, my witchy friend rummaged through the packets of powdered herbs and resins she always kept on hand. "Harmony, harmony, harmony, harmony—bingo. Peace and Harmony." She flicked the packet at me like it was a playing card. I caught it. It held a tea bag.

"Tea?"

"Blessed, made with cleansing herbs and enough chamomile to knock out a longhorn. Get him to drink it and sit with him until he calms down. It won't take him very long but he's gonna be chatty and prone to bad decisions for a bit. You're now ground control."

"Okay." I paused. "Do you have any idea why all this would have hit him so hard?" I said.

"All this what?" Maggie said.

"Camille Ward," I said. "Cops going after the kid that shot her. Him punching Max. I spilled coffee all over both of us and he's acting like he's just been eviscerated."

Maggie closed her eyes and went back to her herb drawers. "Crap. Fuck. Wait there." And she abandoned the enamel chest. Instead, she crouched down in front of a safe. I hadn't known Maggie *had* a safe up here. She even blocked the combination from view as she rummaged through the contents. "Here. This one, too." And she flicked another packet at me.

"What's this one?" I asked. It smelled strongly of mint and felt cold, even though its wrapper.

"Don't ask. Give it to him. He'll know what it is, and he knows he needs it."

Why would Peter have a special tea in Maggie's safe? "Just another question for today, I guess."

"What do you mean?" Maggie said.

"Just…the effect this Camille thing is having on Peter. What am I missing here?" I said.

"The fact that you're *almost* the whitest person in the agency?" Maggie said.

"I get that part. I just feel…blind. There's something here that I don't even have context for, and if I'm going to help Peter…It's not just Camille's death. He's been on like this since before she died."

Maggie nodded. "Part of it is…just being Black. You see people who look like you, or your sister, or your mom and dad, and nobody cares what happens to them, or to you. I mean…I'm Hispanic and my granddad was Black. I'm at the top of my game. I have three doctorates. Objectively I should be some big dollar consultant for a hot-shot law firm. I work here. Dallas's occult expert is a white guy who barely got his master's degree in forensic training. Houston's is a witch who publishes books I correct for her every year. She lives in River Oaks. I live Southside. People like Pete and me have to work twice as hard to get half as far as people like Max and you. And it never stops. And he's right. Anywhere else, he hit somebody like Max, he'd be out the door."

"Race just feels like a cheap answer," I said.

"It is cheap when it doesn't affect you. This isn't part of your life, Astrid. You can't empathize with something you've never experienced. And denial…" She trailed off, prompting me to finish.

"Denial's just a river in Africa. And I'm denying…what, that my perspective is off?" I said.

She nodded, then sighed. "There *is* another part of this. But that's not my story to tell. And right now I don't think it's yours to hear."

"But I want to understand. I want to do the right thing—"

Maggie held up a hand, stopping my ever-running mouth before it could dig the hole much deeper. "No. What you want is satisfaction, Stone. But you're not entitled to it. This is a boundary that Peter needs you to respect. You want to help? You listen to what he says. I mean, really listen, not just wait for your chance to talk. Don't ask him to give more than what he has."

"But how is *asking* him what's wrong…well, wrong?" I said.

"If you're bleeding out you shouldn't have to coach your doctor through the surgery. Pete's about to snap in half. Just be there and do what he needs you to do, and if you don't figure it out…" She sighed. "Go ask somebody else."

I left her office, feeling even less sure than I had been. In fact, I felt dirty. And I felt something looming over both of us, disconnected, a ghost without a haunting. The tension was growing heavy and ripe like fresh fruit, and I had no idea what would happen when it finally came time to harvest.

Chapter Five

I brought Peter the tea, the first bag already steeping and the second, colder bag wrapped in a napkin from the coffee stand. As I drew nearer, Domi and the new intern evaporated from his side, leaving him alone. I paused. Closed my eyes. Fuck me if I knew how to handle this. But unloading my discomfort on him was going to be the wrong thing to do. So I drew in a deep breath, plastered on a smile that felt fake as last night's Halloween masks, and approached his desk. "Maybe if we hustle, we can do all our paperwork by lunch and go home," I said, trying to sound chipper. I set the tea and the bag on his desk.

Our desks were right next to each other, the dividing wall between them lower than the ones we shared with other desks. We were supposed to be in collaboration, after all. We'd spent a lot of time passing jokes, snacks, spitballs and zingers over that low wall. Peter critiqued my collection of monster movie posters—not even good ones, but classics like *The Blob* and *Plan 9 from Outer Space*. I appreciated his display of vintage records and tossed shade at the hoard of hair care products in his desk drawer.

Peter didn't say anything. His eyes looked flat and dead. He took the tea and added Maggie's secret recipe to the mix with no change of expression.

Okay. That was the wrong approach. I sat down in my chair, wheeled over to the divider and leaned on it. "You wanna talk about it?"

"No," Peter said, turning towards his work. He typed for a minute. Stopped. "Yes, but not with…" He stopped. Looked at me.

"Not with me," I said. It hurt. It shouldn't have hurt, but it did. But I remembered what Maggie told me. I was not what mattered right now. "Okay," I said, and turned to work.

"Look. It's not like that," He said, hastily. As if it were his job to repair my hurt. Because he cared. He *did* care, and that wounded me too. Was our friendship this uneven? He did this much work, and I so much less? And still, he stopped himself. Returned to his own work slowly, like an old machine warming up.

"It's fine. I'm the one fucking up here. I should be here for you the way you've been for me and…" I paused, gathering my thoughts.

"Maggie gave you the 'shut up and listen speech?'" He said.

Damn it. "Maybe." I said.

He chuckled and drank tea. "She gave me and half the office a slightly different version when you got dumped by Mr. Ghost."

I'd been married, once, and I couldn't tell anymore if it had been a sweet halcyon dream or a nightmare dressed up in china patterns and bed linens. But the ending had been catastrophic by anyone's definition. We hadn't had a fight. I hadn't even noticed a problem. I came home and found the deed to the house, his name removed. He'd left behind his keys, his identification and all his things. And that *hurt*. Having the office spread that pain around like a racoon in the garbage would have just tripled that ache. But I hadn't known that Maggie was the reason our gossipmongers had been shut down.

That made me smile, just a tad.

Peter still looked like his dog had died. "We could go down to training and you could hit me for a while." I said. I could muddle through basic forms with the best of them, but Peter excelled at hand-to-hand, with high-ranking belts in two disciplines. Our training sessions usually resulted in him mopping most of the gym with me in the name of teaching. It was fun, sometimes.

He put his head in his hands. Sat there for a few moments, just breathing. I waited. I was about to give up and start typing names into our fillable forms when he began to talk.

"I'm just so goddamn *tired*," he said.

Voices drifted around us, and the ringing of phones, the clatter-clack of keyboards. A river of work, in which we were an isolated stone. I kept my mouth shut. I listened.

He began rubbing his hands together. "I gotta respect her," He said. "Camille. She's the client." He paused, breathing like a man on the top of a precipice, looking down. "Astrid, she knew me. First time she saw me. She knew things she shouldn't." Another pause. His hands began to shake. He stopped. Swallowed.

"What did she know?" I asked.

He just shook his head, over and over. Frantic, as if he were warding off a ghost. Maybe, with those specific words, he was. Fragments of the news drifted towards us, shards of poisoned glass. *Pillar of her community—warrior for vampiric rights—civil rights leader. Amazing loss. Amazing loss. What a blow to history.*

Peter got up, walked to his wastebasket, and stood there for a few minutes. Fighting the urge to vacate, to purge. He closed his eyes, gulping air. "I gotta do something." He whispered. "I can't just let this happen again."

I handed him a water bottle and a napkin. "Look. Maggie said you're probably going to be a bad-idea machine for a little bit after this."

"On that tea? Yep." Peter said.

I should have encouraged him to sit down and do nothing. That would have kept both of us safe. But "safe" could go jump off a pier. "What's the worst idea you can think of right now?" I said.

He thought for a minute. Then his balled up nervous tension smoothed out into purpose. "Go find that little boy before this turns into a lynch mob."

"Okay." Deep breath. Take the plunge. "Then let's go find him." I said.

His brows rose in surprise. "You're serious, Stone?"

"I cover your ass if you'll cover mine," I said, and reached for my coat.

"It's a terrible idea," Peter said.

"Horrible. The exact thing Maggie doesn't want me to do. I can always sit down and forget. You can too. Ding, dong, the witch is dead. Our lives can just go on like it never happened."

He closed his eyes, as if in pain.

And then he grabbed his coat.

Chapter Six

The little boy who shot Camille was mixed race, Black and white. That was what the news said, in between clips about how Camille had been a beautiful historical treasure. Gag me. The little boy's name was Joseph Harris. The television featuring his image sat on a yellowed 70s era end table at his grandmother's house. We'd been given her address by the cops, and she'd permitted our entry Above the words *killer tot,* the news showed one solemn picture of him in the arms of his dad. I suppose they had picked the most mugshot-esque photo they could find of a toddler. His mother was very white, very blonde, and the photo they used from her social media showed a well-dressed woman, long hair, designer sunglasses, a glass of champagne saluting the camera. Her name was Julia. When they talked about her they used words like "caregiver fatigue" and "ambitious single mother". Joseph they called "juvenile". The word "delinquent" was left unsaid, but it hung off the back of the other word, doing a lot of heavy lifting for something so quietly unsaid.

The grandmother's home was a small two bedroom on the west side of Crosstown Expressway, closer to the refineries than the lights and shops along South Padre Island Drive. It looked very 70s, by way of the 90s. Green pile carpet and yellowed plastic furniture that had been lovingly cared for. Clear plastic covers on the pale, wood-legged furniture; they crinkled when I sat down. This home smelled like sage and sausage and love.

Facing us down as if we were dragons rampaging her collection of dark skinned Precious Moments figurines (Set up in a left hand corner in a multi-tiered Ikea display, atop a very impressive collection of crocheted doilies) was a small, old Black woman, weathered face and white hair, in a seersucker housecoat and fluffy bunny slippers that read "Best Grandma". She rocked in a chair in the corner and had not said one word to us.

Grandma Harris appeared to love three things: crochet, small bible-themed ceramics and her grandson. Above the television were nearly a hundred other images, the boy fleshed out and made real. Two feet by three feet in a frame over the mantle, a tiny baby with big eyes and a thrilled smile. Wallet sized and set in tiny frames, his advancement through Sunday School and pre-k. Smiling at the camera, head up, eyes back. He liked dress up. He liked race cars. There was a sand table filled with dinosaurs and farm toys, a t-rex hitched up to a plow. Creative. Intelligent.

It was easy, I thought, to make someone fit your prompt words when you choose just one picture. I wondered how often *killer tot* would appear onscreen if the news desks had to use this plethora of memories. Funny. In all of this, no one had once shown the image of Camille handing the gun to the baby.

Mrs. Harris crocheted granny squares unironically. Beside her, a basket with ten different skeins of yarn and nearly thirty neat, multicolored squares waited to recieve her next creation. She glared at us without once pausing; her work was flawless. It reminded me of a nun praying a rosary. Hail Mary, full of grace, five double crochets in each two-chain space, the Lord is with thee, five double crochet, chain two, five more, turn the corner. Occasionally she looked at the images of her grandson and her fingers picked up their pace. She'd finished two squares while pointedly not talking to us. Now she tied off this one and started another, wordlessly. We'd come here to ask questions about Joe, and I'd had hope for assistance when she let us in, but she neither spoke to us nor answered questions. Her eyes glimmered with wet. Her cheeks were perfectly dry.

She was halfway through her third square when her screen door banged open.

"Mamma, I swear I can't get them to tell me a damn…" The man saw us as he came in the door and stopped talking.

"You don't talk to cops," she said. "You hear me Bobby? They want to find him, they do that on their own."

Frustrated, I said, "All due respect, ma'am, why'd you even let us in the building?"

She pointed behind us with her crochet hook. "Because you call my Joey a killer. You come in here and can't see that, you're blind."

Bobby Harris. The boy's father. Robert was what the news reports had said. I guess it sounded harsher. He wore a Valero jacket and looked like a man who worked hard. Worn, I think, worn like the fit of old shoes. A couple marks on his face made me think welder. They were the right size and place for a mask. His hair was cropped against his scalp, and his face had a whole 747's worth of baggage. The desperation in his eyes nearly came with its own contact high. He sighed, defeated. "You cops?" He said.

"Terrestrial Affairs," I said.

"Oh…the Fairy-tale cops," Bob's shoulders slumped.

"We don't have arrest authority," I said.

"Don't matter how nice they look, Bobby. They're cops." Grandma Harris said.

"Ms. Harris," I started to say.

In the same beat, Peter said, "Astrid, maybe you'd better wait outside."

"What?" I said.

He just looked at me. Not even an attempt to pretend like he wasn't kicking me out. I opened my mouth and closed it as my brain canvassed a thousand retorts…and came up empty.

Grandma Harris said, "I don't care which one of you leaves. Far as I care, you're both crackers to me."

"Momma—" Mr. Harris began to say.

"You keep your mouth shut." She said. "You ever want to see that boy alive again you just keep your fuckin' mouth shut. You know what they do."

Okay. Well, there was a clear chance to divide and conquer here. Except when I started to speak, Peter stopped me again. "Astrid. Go outside."

"But—"

"It's not about you," he said.

It wasn't about me. He didn't mean, me leaving, because that absolutely *was* about me. He meant this whole situation. My satisfaction, hell, even my involvement, were completely superfluous. And if I wasn't helping, I needed to leave.

"Okay, Pete." I said. I tried not to grit my teeth as I walked away.

Emphasis on *tried*.

Outside. Was it even noon yet? The sky was overcast and cloudy. I could have checked my watch but on all-nighters I almost prefer the unreality of sleep deprivation over something like concrete time keeping. The dazed, almost high feeling helped me ignore how very much I wanted to just go to *bed*. To keep busy, I tried to "read" the Harris's front yard. You can tell a lot about somebody by how they live. This yard could have been neater. The grass was worn, especially around a four-foot tree stump, mushrooms growing out of the front. Someone had put faux flowers and a toy dinosaur into each of the rotting holes where branches used to be. Weeds grew in clumps between patches of hard packed earth. The flower bed nearest the house was well tended. The one under the flower box, not so much. There were toy dinosaurs there too. A bike with training wheels lay on its side.

I liked that the yard was not perfectly neat, that the grass had been worn down. Appearances mattered less than the ten thousand games of tag that had been played around that stump. Toys were scattered because they were moments on pause. And they were *still* here because they were also a promise. When Joe got back, he would pick up where he left off. *When,* not if. I had no doubt whose will it was dictating this yard clutter. Grandma was a force for good.

The sad thing was how untrue that promise would be. If and when somebody found Joseph Harris, his life would be different, forever. Even if we got him back in one piece, even *if* he avoided any legal repercussions for this—which he should. He *was* only five—he'd always remember that he killed that pretty blonde lady.

Funny. This was the first real quiet moment I'd had since we found Camille's ashes and that part just felt...unreal. No, not even *unreal, not* real. It seemed very neat, very tidy. Pretty blonde lady hands over gun, little black boy uses it. Kind of...prepackaged to do...well, exactly what it *was* doing. Get the whole world onto Camille's side.

I went to the garden and saw a few low stones inlaid with mosaic pieces. One of them said *I heart Grandma*. Another one had a large tree in a round frame. Both were by the same artist. I recognized the tree; that was the Big Tree, a thousand-year-old live oak in Goose Island state park.

I remembered the peroxide Marilyn Monroe, Camille's neighbor with the cameras. Her voice, heavy with the stink of Opium floated up like bad dreams: *She was from another time, you understand. They didn't have all this confusion about guns and…and…and back then they valued their Second Amendment rights.* I touched the shoulder where that woman had gripped me, her French manicure digging into my skin. *Train them up early. That would have been her motto, back in the day.*

Peter had been right. Camille *would* have known better. I turned the Big Tree mosaic around in my fingers, trying to follow the nebulous idea to its genesis.

That gut-clenching feeling of watching Camille face to face with both mother and son. Could she have rolled Joe? Or maybe a better question was *why* would she roll Joe? Suicide by toddler? Why not just eat a hamburger?

Because you can't come back from that, I thought, and inhaled. No. It was stupid. It was crazy. The world was so much better with her dead. But the thought just wouldn't go away.

I took my cell phone and dialed.

"Magdalena," Maggie answered.

"Are you still at work?" I said.

"The day after Rabies night I'm always at work. What gives?" She said.

"I know you said there isn't a way to confirm Camille's ashes are hers," I began.

"There isn't a *court admissible* way to identify them without me having to drag out some really big guns, which we don't need. Or…didn't need. Why?"

"How long would it take to check if court admission isn't a concern?" I said.

"About as long as it takes for me to draw and quarter a circle. *Why?*"

"I dunno. I got a feeling."

"You got a feeling. You want me to put on a horse and pony show on your feelings?" She said.

"Yes." I said. And meant it.

There were a few beats of silence, and then Maggie sighed. "Well. Maybe I had my own feeling. Maybe I already got all the stuff out to do it and was trying to talk myself out of looking stupid. What sat wrong with you?"

"She's a hundred-fifty-year old Southern Girl. She would know better than to let a kid play with her six shooter."

"It was a Glock automatic," Maggie said. "Alright. Give me about ten, fifteen minutes and I'll confirm that our Golden Girl is the one in the vacuum."

And she hung up.

"Something wrong?" A voice over my head. I looked up into Bob Harris's aching brown eyes.

"Just Agency stuff. Big Tree, huh?" I held up the mosaic.

"Yeah. We went there all the time. At least, before me and his mom broke up. Proper introduction. Robert Harris. Joe's Dad. Dragon lady's son."

I shook his offered hand. It was warm and rough from hard work. He moderated his grip until he got a good measure of mine. I liked him. "Astrid Stone. Agent Stone. Sometimes people need dragons." I nodded. "It's nice out at the Big Tree. Peaceful. Sometimes you feel like you can just lean back and hear the trees talk." I wasn't going to push.

Bob sat down on his porch and pulled out his cigarettes. Lit one. Blew out a long plume of smoke. Said, "Mom can be a bit harsh with strangers. Don't take it personally."

I shrugged. "With what you guys are going through, she's earned the right to breathe fire at me."

He studied his cigarette for a minute. Deciding. "What happened? Cops won't tell us anything except my boy shot this woman."

Protocol could go screw itself. I told him, replaying those moments in my head. The wrongness seemed to get more vivid. "We've got it on tape. It looks like he was posing with a toy from his costume, and Camille decided to give him the real thing and…well, he's four. That's why you don't give a gun to a baby."

Bob nodded. "What about his mom? Julia should have been with him."

"She was. She was standing right next to him when it happened. She picked him up and ran off. Cops have an APB out for him. Peter…doesn't trust it." I paused. "And maybe I don't either."

"That's what scares me." He said, and stubbed out the cigarette.

I wanted to say something about how nothing could possibly happen to his child, but I kept my mouth shut. I didn't want to say what I didn't believe. Even if this situation was just what it said on the tin…and I had my doubts now, didn't I?

Bob Harris was scared. You didn't have to be a psychic to see that. It stood out in his sweat, glistening on muscles and in his hair. It was in the way he smoked, too, desperately sucking on coffin nails as if it was oxygen. His eyes kept searching the street, darting back and forth.

"You *can* talk to him, you know. Peter hated Camille's guts. He'd probably give your son a medal if we had one to give." I said.

Bob shrugged. "Mom's got the right of it. I shouldn't even be out here but…I want to *do* something, damn it. Joey and Julia are *out there*." He gestured, and it encompassed the world, every danger highlighted in neon. "It's eating me up, inside."

"You and his mom together?" I asked.

"Us? No." He pressed his lips together into a fine line and tears threatened in his eyes. But there was more anger than sadness here. "She'd joke about how she liked herself that dark meat. Took me a while to figure out it wasn't much of a joke. I'd do it again, though, just to get that boy. I swore to God I'd keep him safe and it feels like I've done nothing but break that promise. I weld at night and stay up all day cause I just wanna hear that little boy laugh. Mom watches him because we're both working. Couldn't get last night off, so I told her to take him without me. God, I knew better."

"He's a cute kid," I said. There were other questions I should ask, like *where do you think your ex would go* and *does she have any family in the area*. But if Peter deserved space and deference right now, Bob Harris deserved more. This was his kid. "He got a dinosaur thing?"

Bob nodded. The motion ran down, a motor on fumes. "You think you and your partner can get him back safe?"

I frowned. Took a deep breath. "Yesterday I would have said yes. Today…today I don't know. A lot of stuff I thought I could trust, I'm figuring out that I can't. I—"

And that was when Bob's phone rang.

Chapter Seven

"Oh thank God," he said, and hit the green button. "Julie, you tell me where my baby is. You tell me right…" He stopped, and seemed to pale around the edges, gaining a yellowish gray color that quickly flushed out as his eyes grew wide. After a few heartbeats, in a voice shaking with some kind of nameless terror, he said, "Julia. Julia. You're not making any sense. Jules…" He trailed off. Looked at me, motioned me closer, and hit the speaker button.

"--death rather than living torment? To die is to be banish'd from myself; And Julia is myself: banish'd from her is self from self: a deadly banishment! What light is light, if Julia be not seen? What joy is joy, if Julia be not by? Unless it be to think—"

He muted our end. "I don't get it," he said. "Is she drunk?"

It was a woman's voice, and I recognized the words as Shakespeare. Except the name was wrong. I'd covered that speech in high school. That was Proteus's speech from *Two Gentlemen of Verona,* in which Proteus forgets

45

his first love and becomes something of an ass to the second—I'd always felt that play best ended with the more heroic male lead and the two girls beating the absolute snot out of Proteus before running off to form a threesome. But more distressing than the words was how they were spoken. A robot would have more emotion. And they were rushed, one spilling out from another as rapidly as possible.

"Is that your ex's voice?"

"Yeah, that's Julia."

The two female characters in the play were Julia and Silvia. Julia was the love that Proteus forgot. The name in the speech was Sylvia, the love he chose. Someone *could* be sending us a fancy message, but I doubted it, because of the way Julia was speaking.

She hadn't paused once. Not even for breath. Half of her words were spoken as she inhaled. I'd only heard someone speak like this once, during a safety workshop. One of the more human-friendly vampires we worked with came in and rolled a volunteer to show us what vampires can and cannot do. They can make you sit, stand, dance and recite the Pledge of Allegiance if you already have it memorized, but they don't have enough control to put words in your mouth that aren't already in your head.

One of the things our classes recommend is that if you are rolled and forced to speak, you say the most off-the-wall thing you can think of in line with their command.

"Did Julia ever do drama classes? Acting? Study Shakespeare?" I said.

"Yeah…huh. I think I know that speech. It's the one where she always got the name wrong. She thought it was her own."

So here's the scenario: Somebody rolled Julia Harris and ordered her to dial her ex. Great. But now she has to identify herself over the phone, and we don't typically store our identities as rote speech. The vampire goes with whatever floats to the top of Julia's mind. And by floating Proteus's romantic whining, Julia had just demonstrated that she was one smart cookie.

Still, I needed to test this. Fortunately, our training covered that, too.

Vampires are somewhat allergic to religion. *Their own* religion. Typically, the very religious in life don't turn, but someone with vague ties to a faith will find those connections metamorphosized into unbreakable chains of devotion. What was holy in life become anathema in death. This doesn't necessarily indicate any one religion is more valid. A vampire dabbling in Heathenry will recoil from Odin's iconography the same way an undead

Christian responds to a cross. What makes this a sometimes thing is that Atheist and Agnostic vampires are immune. The good news was that vampire demographics—the White Anglo-Saxon Protestant majority—made Christocentric religion a safe bet, most of the time.

The rest of the time padded undertaker college funds.

Of course, holy water, crosses, the host and rosaries don't exactly translate through a cell phone. That left us with one potential way to pry this vampire's fingers off Julia Harris's mind.

"Pray. Something really sacred."

"I ain't all that good of a Christian, miss," Harris said.

"It's not your faith that matters. It's hers."

"Julia ain't much of one either," He said, but he unmuted the call. And he did pray. The Lord's prayer, the words simple and unadorned and yet in his voice, backed by fear, they held power.

But I was focused more on my slip of the tongue.

Hers. I was referring to the vampire, not Julia. As much as I'd like to be different, I was the kind of person who assumes the defaults: male, white, Christian, English-speaking, and so on. I try to be better about it, but "try" doesn't always translate to "do". But here, in the heat of the moment, I had assumed female. And I really did not like that.

Because I'd already had doubts about Camille Ward's death.

Not that it couldn't be another female vampire. I just hadn't thought that Camille had any fledglings loyal enough to avenge her death; she certainly hadn't had any devoted enough to follow her to Corpus.

About the time I thought a vampire would recognize the prayer, Julia stopped reciting Shakespeare and began screaming. High and long and loud, with a bare pause for breath before screaming again.

"Don't stop praying, Bob. Julia! Julia, I'm with Terrestrial—"

She didn't even give me enough time to finish. "Help me! She's got me and Joe! We're at the pier!"

And then the phone call cut off. The quiet after those screams was deafening.

"What the fuck was that?" Bob said.

"It's what happens when a vampire rolls somebody and then makes them use a telephone." I ran up the porch steps and almost slammed the door open. Grandma Harris stared at me as if I had just taking a dump on the green shag carpet. "You got some nerve—" She began.

"A vampire has Julia and Joe. They just made her puppet back Shakespeare over the phone."

"What vampire?" Peter said.

"I don't know. Maybe Camille had a lacky. We can get Maggie on that part. There's got to be a way to confirm those ashes belong to Ward. But if we have a baby in the hands of a vampire willing to risk daywalking—"

"We gotta go." Peter said. "You got a clue where?"

I shook my head. "She just said, 'the pier'. 'We're at the pier'." This was the coast. There must be a fishing pier every hundred yards on the bayfront. She might as well have said *we're at the tree.*

Bob said, "You let me come with you, I'll tell you where the pier is."

"We can't endanger civilians," I said.

In the same moment, Peter said, "Go get in the car."

"Pete," I said.

He completely ignored me. Instead, Peter crossed to the old lady, knelt in front of her with the nobility and purpose of a knight bowing to his liege, and clasped her hands in his. "We *are* going to find your grandson. I promise. And I will bring him home alive."

He hauled me out of the living room, partially out of well-justified haste. But mostly because we both knew he made a promise none of us could keep.

Chapter Eight

"Alright. What pier?" Peter said.

"Head to Lamar," Mr. Harris said. "That's where we went all the time as a family. Even when Julia was going off me, when we do family stuff, we go to Lamar. It's the one place where I'd always know where to find her. Anywhere else, she'd have named the town."

Peter and I exchanged a glance. That wasn't the kind of thing you'd volunteer under vampiric manipulation if there wasn't something else involved. I liked this situation less and less. We clearly were not in charge of it.

"So. The question I have is, is this Camille herself, or did Camille have a minion we didn't know about?" Peter asked.

A vampire's power grows with two factors: their age and their lineage. That Camille made it to a hundred-fifty and apparently had no fledglings said some pretty expansive things about her personality, none of them positive. Turning a fledgling requires a lot of self control—both to not kill your victim until they're guaranteed to turn, and to keep them alive long enough for them to boost your power.

"We gotta make sure Camille is dead." Peter said.

"On it," I said, and dialed Maggie. She answered on the first ring. That's never a good sign.

"Mija, don't take this the wrong way, but where the *fuck* are you two?" She said.

"Nice to hear you too," I said. "What's the problem?"

She said, "I'm standing here with a bombshell on my hands looking at Peter's desk and he only drank half his tea. So I repeat: Where the *fuck* are you?"

"Lemme guess. You tested those ashes and they're not Camille's." I said.

There were a few moments of silence. "Before I say one more thing, Astrid Stone, I want you to tell me that you and Peter are down at the *Laughing Gull* getting drunk off your collective asses in solidarity."

"Something like that." I said. "So who is it, if it's not Cam?"

Peter began to swear. Really colorful things, in which the word *fuck* and *fucking* were employed with the creative artistry of a maestro.

"I'm not sure, because she had no leftover belongings, but one of your missing persons from Sanctuary House is a dead ringer for the lady." Maggie said. "We widen the net to state-wide, there's a couple more missing fangs who fit the bill. It would have been easy for her to find a body double if she wanted. But those ashes definitely are not hers."

"How'd you test that?" Peter said. He was driving as if we could zoom into a time travel portal with 80s fashion sense. "You can't DNA test vamp remains."

"Right, but there are other options. Not quite court admissible without certification, which is why my salary is bigger than yours. Sympathetic magic." Maggie said.

"That's where you like…dye a piece of onion in a magic circle and the rest of the onion turns blue?" I said.

"Yep. We found a hair sample of hers on a brush. I dunked it in holy water to see if the ashes got wet."

Oh *shit*. "Within the last ten minutes?" I said.

"About."

"Would a living vampire have felt that?" I said.

There were a few seconds of silence, then Maggie began to swear. She was better at it than Peter. More languages to pull from. "I'm an idiot. I'm sorry. I was thinking about confirming it was Cam, not what Cam would—"

"Got it. Thanks Mags." And Peter grabbed the phone, hung up on her before she could say anything else. The phone began buzzing nearly immediately. I turned it off, then fished Peter's out of his coat. It got to ring once before I turned that one off.

"She's gonna be pissed," I said.

"You're welcome to keep her updated," Peter said.

"You guys weren't doing this for the agency, were you?" Bob said.

"Sort of," Peter said.

"Pete, I'm not worried about *Maggie* being pissed. That timing—"

"I know it," Peter said. He sounded very tired. "That test would have happened right before Julia called Harris here, right?" Peter said.

"Speaking of me being here, I'm not following this conversation real well." Bob said.

I twisted around in my seat, as far as my seatbelt would allow. "There's a chance your son is off the hook. The only proofs we have that Camille Ward is actually dead are her ashes in a hallway and a really shitty security camera from across the street. Our witch friend just tested the ashes and it doesn't look like they're hers."

"But the way she tested it, Camille would have felt it." Peter said.

"Yeah, that would have felt like…what, to her?" I asked.

"A full body dunking in holy water. Wouldn't have done her any permanent damage but it would have hurt like a sonofabitch." He paused, then grinned. "Somebody call Peter Pan, 'cause that's my new happy thought."

"I thought vampires couldn't be active during the day." Harris said.

"They can't go out in sunlight. It gives them contact burns. But there's ways for a vampire to day-walk if they want to." Peter said.

"Blackout suits," I added. "They're priced out of most vampires' range but Camille has stupid money. She could still be dead," I said.

"You sure you weren't being Pollyanna last night?" Peter said.

Neither of us had changed out of costume. "I can call Maggie back and see if Camille had a reason to fake her death."

"Maggie's smart, Astrid. If she hasn't already pulled everything from Camille's financials to her gynecological exam, I'll eat my phone. We check in once the kid's safe," He said.

"I hate to suggest this—" I said.

"Then *don't.*" Peter tightened his grip on the wheel.

"If we called the police they could probably get a GPS location on Julia's phone."

"Not without a warrant, not in time, and not without handing them that little boy all gift-wrapped like a present."

"But if Camille's alive—"

"They won't care." Peter said.

"But—"

"Do you want to help with this?" He said. I'd never heard my friend so cold. "Because I can drop you off and you can get the boss to untangle things, and you can call the cops while I go try to actually rescue this kid."

"I want to help." I said.

"Then that means that for once in your goddamn life, you shut up, sit down and listen," he said.

Silence, save for the noise of the car driving over the highway.

"Shutting up," I said, and Peter got onto the Crosstown exit ramp leading to Portland.

Lamar was an unincorporated township just a little north of Rockport-Fulton. Nearly forty-five minutes away from Corpus when your driver follows the speed limit. Peter had ignored this into non-existence. I grabbed the car's oh-shit handle above the passenger window as he blew through Portland, slowing only when he neared speed traps I had never even registered before. His hands were steady on the wheel, clenched so tight I could almost smell of faux leather melting under friction. Fields alternated between milo and cotton, the latter in various stages of harvest. White mounds lined the road like snowdrifts.

None of us said "Everything might be fine". We were all in agreement that it wouldn't be.

You don't realize how much time it takes to go somewhere until you can't move fast enough. Every second pressed against skin, as if against glass. And everything was gray. Usually there was enough color to fill a whole artist's palette. The wide blue sky, the endless procession of grasses. Meadows, farmland, dune grass on the island heading up towards home. But when the sky is overcast the world reduces to asphalt, the live oaks darkening to a green barely more than black. And the sea answers it, echoes it. But now with the overcast skies, it was a gray world caught on a breath between life and death, and we were racing towards a single moment in it. Don't breathe, this world seemed to say. Don't risk it.

Rockport, Texas, has a population of ten thousand, with another thousand-and-change in Fulton. The two towns together are something of a combination art colony and tourist draw. There's a lot of wealth in Key Allegro, and a lot of poverty everywhere else. Downtown is full of eclectic junk shops and art galleries. Restaurants are all the sort reviews call "hidden gems" or "watering holes with character." This translates to either expensive with fancy décor, or expensive with wood paneling and buckets of peanuts you can throw on the floor. I think the peanuts are the "character". The artist colony rents out pottery wheels and studio space, and the annual art fair every fourth of July is a square filled with their best efforts. It's all rainbow bright colors papered over desperation. It's a town that tries its best in a world with no rewards.

Lamar was over the three-mile causeway stretching across the mouth of Copano Bay like a necklace on a throat. The water there is restless, streaked with silt from the Gulf of Mexico. The bay is rimmed by a low forest of live oaks. The trees lean away from the bay, driven by wind and salt in postcard perfect imagery. There's a pier that runs nearly the full length of the causeway, one of the more popular fishing spots in the area. I always glanced at it when I drove past, even if I was just in the passenger seat. It was something of a landmark.

Which was why I saw her. Julia Harris, holding her boy and standing on the pier's railing, right where the bay goes deep. I recognized her by her scrubs and the bright red vest her son wore on his shoulders. His cowboy hat was long gone. First one on the way into town. Might as well have been on a billboard.

"There they are." I said, quickly, and pointed.

Peter cursed. "I can't turn on the goddamn causeway. We're gonna have to go around." He somehow coaxed a little bit more speed out of the sedan and we nearly flew down the rest of the street. This had to be unsafe, but I wasn't going to protest. "She's not even *trying* to be subtle," he muttered.

I was more concerned about how *still* that pier was. Why wasn't anyone trying to get Mrs. Harris off the rail? There were *always* people fishing down there. Seeing a woman teetering on the railing over the deep end, kid in her arms, should have been an instant 911 call. Three miles up. That image, the woman on the rail, felt burned into my retinas. The causeway guardrail ticked by, flashes of the silver-green water below, and the ten thousand bad things that could happen kept building themselves up in my mind. Peter slowed long enough to make a barely safe turn in a Texaco parking lot, and now it was three miles back, each yard gaping longer than the ocean's hungry maw. It took so much *time.*

Now I had a near perfect view of the pier. It waivered in and out of sight, blocked frequently by the guardrails, but the picture clarified. It was, indeed, busy. There were at least fifteen people sitting there. *Sitting*, as a woman stood on the pier railing. The ever-present costal wind whipped her hair into a golden froth. Joe's legs and arms hung very still, his head cupped on his mother's shoulders.

I felt sick.

Mr. Harris gasped, a brief intake like he'd been punched. "No," he said, short and sharp.

"It might not be what it looks like," I said, feeling cold.

"What?" Peter said. "What do you see?"

"He's too still," Mr. Harris said. "It looks like she's got—"

"Wait." I said, to him. "Not yet. Not until you have him in your arms. Don't you give up on him yet." To Peter, "Julia is standing on the rail. She's got the kid in her arms. He's real still. Could be sleeping. Maybe drugs. But Pete…there's fifteen people—sixteen…seven—there's a bunch. There's a lot of people on that pier and *nobody* is doing anything."

Vampires *can* roll more than one person. It's like juggling, apparently. After they reach a certain age, a certain flexibility of magic and will, they can nearly all manage one person. As they grow in power, they can add more people to the game. But each one takes extra concentration. You must think about all of them, all at once. The ability to hold that many people on the dock? There weren't a lot of vampires in that weight bracket, at least not down here in South Texas.

Camille was one of them.

Peter's hands tightened on the wheel.

"It still could be someone else." I said.

Peter said nothing. In silence, Peter said everything.

We parked in the small lot in front of the pier. "Stay in the car, Mr. Harris—" Peter said.

But he got out before we could stop him. He ran up the asphalt parking lot, his Valero jacket flaring out like the wings of an avenging angel. His child was up there, and a woman he had loved. Nothing, I think, could have held him back.

"Shit," Peter cursed, and both of us got out of the car as quick as we could. Mr. Harris could move, I thought, as we raced past pickups full of fishing gear, a bike rack loaded down with bikes.

"We'll catch him at the—" *admission booth*, I was going to say, but he blew past that without protest. Someone *should* have stopped him. I couldn't see from here, but that booth should have been occupied. And if it wasn't, the admission gate should have been closed and locked.

And so we ran too, full out. It didn't require communication. We both knew a municipal attraction refusing money was a bad sign. The small, squat building existed as little more than a combination cashier's office and toilet. If it wasn't fulfilling part of its purpose, something must be very wrong.

Up close, we got confirmation. The admissions guy stood square in the double window, dead still. He wore a blue *City of Rockport/Fulton* shirt, logo screen-printed onto his breast pocket. Neat hair, his hand extended into the half open window, a smile on his lips. He'd been caught in a greeting, I suspected. He wasn't dead. His chest rose and fell. Drool escaped the corner of his mouth and tears poured from his unblinking eyes. He had been standing here, frozen, for so long that his own fluids had soaked into his shirt from collar to mid-chest. He was in thrall, rolled by a vampire who wasn't playing nice.

You didn't *have* to lock down a thrall's entire body to the point that you stole their eyelids and made them drool. Whoever had done this liked the aesthetics of suffering. Like dressing up in crinolines and your favorite big, fluffy hat when you were going to fake your death. If that's what she'd done.

The gate, made of wood planks and hurricane fencing, sat open. Harris had gone through it already. I let Peter go in first, me right on his heels. The people on the dock had been rolled just like the admissions guy. A small old man at the first fishing bench was frozen, hand on the reel. The broken filament of his fishing line spun in the breeze like spider-silk. The woman and children next to him were also frozen, their hands extended. Their faces were joyful, but tears poured down their cheeks in unrelenting streams and one of the children had soiled themselves, the stain dark on their magenta leggings. Further on, further down, more people frozen as in ice, stripped of dignity as well as volition. And the final kicker that this was for our benefit: Mrs. Harris standing high on the railing with her son in her arms.

She'd done this. She'd walked down the pier and taken every person in turn. Start with the attendant. Freeze. Now the old man, a hand on a shoulder, frozen. The children and mother stopped one at a time. Everyone taken in relative peace, their passive tranquility just part of her show. It had to be hell inside their heads. I had to imagine they were all fighting, beating spiritual wings against the bars of a cage that had been formed of their own nerves and bones. And I had no time to waste on that image, none at all, because there was a woman standing on the rail with a child in her arms, and god only knew when the demented monster who had put her up there was going to pull the strings and send her into the water.

Her long blond hair seemed to blend into the clouds. Royal purple scrubs stood out against the gray like a brand. She clasped her son against her breast, the heart's-blood red of his vest another beacon in this dull noontime light. His sneakers sparkled where they hit her legs. They were happy, the bright things you bought a toddler when you planned to run in the dark. Red and green lights, blinking in sequence. Hope in a pair of shoes. They bounced off his mother's impotent thighs. Hope betrayed.

Mr. Harris made it halfway to her, shouting her name, "*Julie! Julia!*"

And then he stopped. Frozen.

His momentum carried him forward, but his body was not permitted to compensate for motion. He had reached for his ex in his last voluntary movement, so his outstretched fingers broke his fall. He was not permitted to even catch himself. He remained in a runner's stance as his body hit the ground.

A gull's cry broke the silence. It sounded like laughter.

No doubt about it. She was here.

Chapter Nine

Peter and I both dropped behind the nearest bench, our backs to the tableau. The vampire had to be on the far end of the pier to have an eye-line to Harris. The vampire was there, and the vampire had waited. She would have had eye-lines to us too, until the moment we hit the deck. She'd taken Harris first because she'd wanted us to watch.

Enthralled makes this sound magical. Calling it rolled gives you the impression it's like being drugged, with blunted awareness and distance from sensations like pleasure or pain. But the reality is more brutal. When someone is rolled by a vampire, there is no dampening of conscious perception. A vampire can make someone act like they are happy. They can even force the body into a numb arousal, like the involuntary friction that brings forth an erection. But they cannot make someone feel anything. Not without consent. Every adult on this pier was fully and painfully aware. Mrs. Harris, standing on that high, tall rail. Mr. Harris, toppled like an ebony statue. It looked as if some of his fingers had broken. They were twisted, swelling and purple. And still he made no sound. Julia Harris was shaking with the effort to balance on that rail. She swayed with every breath of wind. Every one of them knew that they were captive to someone else's will. They would feel every moment of her unshakable power.

We were on opposite sides of the pier. Peter pressed his back up against his, the rough wood crumpling his coat against his shoulders. His hair had worked loose and it swirled around his shoulders, a stain of dark red against the sky. His eyes closed and he whispered something. It might have been prayers. Above him a older couple, retirees out to enjoy a blustery day, sat and wept involuntary tears. My own bench was unoccupied. I risked a glance backwards, eyes to the ground, and saw her. She'd stepped out into the middle of the pier, looking exactly the way I expected. Dark, melodramatic fabric covered every inch of her silhouette. Big round hat with a thick veil that wrapped around her neck, the better to appreciate her jawline. Long black gloves that lead into long black sleeves. The skirt of her gown was curiously deflated, presumably made for petticoats she hadn't worn. It felt eerily like a costume for a play. She'd turned this pier into her stage.

"This id a trap," Peter said.

"Yeah." And then because I couldn't help it, "For you. Specifically."

Peter was Camille's caseworker by her demand. She'd chosen him the way she would any trendy accessory. She knew he was coming last night. She'd set it up so that he would find her ashes. Those moments on the video where she so carefully and obviously made eye contact with Julia Harris. Hadn't I known, in my gut, that she was rolling her victims? She 'd given Mrs. Harris the command to run, given the boy the command to shoot the poor damned soul she'd used as her stand-in. And then? Regroup with her thralls and wait for us. Wait for Peter to find the boy's father, begin putting the pieces together. Had she even gambled that we would test her ashes? Had she been waiting for the shiver of magic over skin? And she might have rushed in creating this confrontation, but she hadn't sourced that blackout costume in the time it took for us to arrive. Maggie's test with the ashes had only advanced her timeline.

But why? Why was Camille doing this? Why was she making these choices? And could we talk her down?

I doubted it. She had arranged for one murder already and there was no guarantee that her track record pre-pardon would be excluded from a trial.

But still, I had to try. That was the obligation this job created. If I didn't have to kill her, I couldn't. Those were the rules.

"Camille?" I shouted. "You know me. It's Astrid Stone. We meet all the time when Peter checks in on you. Why are you doing this?"

Silence. Gull cries. Water slapping against the pilings beneath us, wind whistling through the railing and the hum-clack-a-clack of cars over the nearby causeway. Another risky glance back told me she was still there, still poised in a show of quasi-gothic pretension.

"Tell you what!" Peter shouted. "You give us the boy and the woman, and we'll come out and talk."

The wind blew harder. The black dress at the end of the pier billowed out, showing that she'd kept some measure of sanity. She wore sensible boots and what looked like thick black jeans under her flowing blackout skirt. Her hands were down, straight against her sides.

"What do you want?" I shouted. "Please. Nobody else needs to die!"

She laughed.

It was not the laugh of a genteel lady, but of someone taking the plunge into high emotion. Panic. Mania. Or else actual, hysterical delight. She'd done this, after all. After god knew how many decades, she was the one pulling the strings. It had to feel good. Against the pleasure of control, what use was sanity? She laughed, and it spiraled until I got the sense of mountains rising, providing her with the great height required for a cataclysmic crash.

And then the sound I wanted least to hear: Splashing as something impacted the water.

I stood up on reflex because I had to. I had to confirm that it was Julia and her child. Except that had been anticipated. She was there where Julia had stood, hand on the rail. That black shape in the wide hat, yards of darkness whipping around her. Something beneath her hat glowed with faint ruby light.

And then Peter grabbed me, yanked me behind him so hard my teeth clicked together. He got me out before she could roll me and then he faced his most hated client. Head up. Chin square. Eyes straight. He looked her dead in the eye and said, "Hello, Camille."

She went for him. Inevitably. And I watched it happen. His eyes locking, open, unblinking, as every muscle in his body stiffened. There is a stillness and a silence to the enthralled that is something like death.

It would take her time to adapt to juggling so many minds at once. Time that Peter had just bought for me.

I knew my cue when I saw it.

I was angry with him. I would be angrier later, when I had time to think and feel, to consolidate thoughts into words and to scream. But now, here, this moment, a child and his mother depended on me. I had to move. I had to.

I justified abandoning him with those thoughts.

I threw my hand over my eyes as I climbed the rail. Quick vault, up and over, and I was in the air. I was going in the water. No stopping it now. Peter would be alone and I had to hope he was strong, but for the Julia and her child I had to go. The water wasn't going to be enough to break the thrall. Unconsciousness wasn't enough. Julia would not save her own life unless her puppet master ordered her to. Joe would drown in her grasp. I had to go in after her.

More justifications.

The water was hard, like hitting cold concrete. I almost lost my breath and the game right there. I kicked off my shoes, stripped off my coat. Basic water safety 101. Everyone learns it in swim lessons, four years old at the pool. Memory rose in sensory impressions. Smell of chlorine. Skin clammy with sunscreen. A dozen pale bodies struggling through the motions. Kick, Astrid. Kick. The clock was ticking. The water was brown and murky, visibility near zero. It smelled of oil and dead things. I had to keep going. Two lives in my hands. Kick, Astrid. Let the cold and the hunger for air strip away all but itself and the task. Focus. Swim. Kick. Stroke arms. Push through. Try to look. Try to see.

There is nothing to hear underwater. Just the muffled silence of yourself, your own heartbeat in your ears, the strangled rhythm of your own movement in the water. The small noises made in the back of the throat to fight the urge to breathe. All the most basic of biological urges put on hold as the cold, silent dark closes over your head.

And I had something to look for. The darkness of deep water was all-consuming, but there, just a little bit ahead, were lights that I could follow. Betrayed hope: The red and green lights from the child's shoes.

But my lungs couldn't take any more. I went back up. Up to the surface, where I gasped for air. That was a mistake, a nearly fatal one. Because silhouetted against the gray sky was a figure in black. I missed that fatal eye-contact by millimeters. Or maybe it was the blaze of wet hair in my eye. The unforgiving sting of contaminated salt. Maybe a vampire couldn't roll you when your eyes were burning.

No time to think, just to do. Tick tock, on the clock. I couldn't do a thing about the vampire. I had to save Joe. I had to save a four-year-old baby. I had to save Julia. I had no room for perception. Just action.

Breathe. Hold. Down. Go.

The pressure crept up the deeper I got, smothering harsh, and this wasn't safe, dead water. A current ate at me, made me aware how I was not made for swimming. No human is. I was fighting an alien environment that would eat me alive with serpentine envelopment. And before my lungs gave out again, I saw it: The twinkle of red and blue and green from Joe's shoes. The good news was that the current was carrying me down towards them.

The bad news was I'd be fighting it on the way up.

They swelled into view like the apparitions in a nightmare. Julia's pale limbs emerged, sculpting out of the murky salt sea. Her scrubs were shaded midnight down here. Her hair spread free of any constriction, mysterious deep sea weeds winding through the current's path. Her son's form was less clear, demarcated by his bright costume. The sea was already trying to eat him away. Her eyes were wide open, her face puce from her own suffocation. This was no easy, still death. This was enforced.

And her hands clenched tight on the body of her child.

In the long, sleepless nights to follow, the only weapon against self-annihilation was this: I did try to save them both. I did try. In the waking nightmares, the mundane passages where a glimpse of violet cloth or flashing shoes caught my attention, in the years to come when I'd pass by Halloween displays and see some wide brimmed, bright red hat, I would scream that into the void of my own self-hatred, I did try. I grabbed her first because if her grip on the boy was good enough it would have worked. But Julia Harris was not in command of her body, and the undead monster that held her down here demanded that Julia die. She fought me. There was still enough life in her to obey. She was to be the vehicle for her own murder. All choices stripped from her, she had to fight to her own death.

So I grabbed the baby. He was so still, either drugged or rolled into comatose tranquility until unconsciousness claimed him. I grabbed Joe and forced his mother's hands apart. Finger by finger. Knowing as I did how little time they had and that I would not be able to come back. Here in the cold, hungry dark I could not scream. Julia could not beg. She was not even permitted a final word. It was all sacrificed to the will of one who wanted us to suffer for her pleasure.

I'm sorry. I thought.

Julia met my eyes.

She could not let her son go. She could not give him to me. She could not ask me to save him. Inside she must have wanted her son to live, but it did not matter. Camille's will trumped all. Julia could not even close her eyes. But she could see. She held on to consciousness as I pulled her son out of her arms. And when his weight became mine to bear, her eyes rolled back into her head.

Joe was free, but far too limp. And my lungs felt ruptured, they felt on fire. Kick, I thought. Kick for the surface. Kick, Astrid. Kick. Water and hypoxia roared in my ears, spots opening and closing in my vision. Hungry mouths. Roses made of oil. The world shimmered as I drowned in white noise. I wanted to breathe. Oh god, all I wanted to do was breathe.

I reached the air and its sweetness was sharp, cutting. I blacked out those last few seconds, because I don't remember flinging my head back. I don't remember the first, desperate gasps. I just remember coughing because I inhaled half the gulf. The saltwater taste was not unlike blood.

No time to recover, to dwell on what I had just done. Joe wasn't breathing.

Was it safe to give somebody rescue breaths in water? We'd covered regular CPR at work, but not what to do if there was no hard surface. And Peter was up there, somewhere. Alone with the vampire. That was the real danger. The real show. And I had abandoned him to it…and had to continue to leave him up there, alone.

An angry voice whispered, if he'd been there we could have saved them both. Why had he let himself be rolled?

I tilted Joe's head back and gave him two quick breaths. On the second, I was rewarded by a mouthful of water. Again that thought, that it tasted like blood. I spat it out, gave him two more breaths, and then got him onto my chest so I could kick to shore. Compartmentalize. Don't think about how time was running out. Time for Peter. For the others on the dock. And for the woman I had abandoned to die.

Why hadn't Peter come with me?

I abandoned her. I had reasons and justifications but that is still what I did. I kicked to shore, alive. She drowned. I should go back. I should find a way to get her too, but I didn't see how. Rescue breaths for her son, from my lungs to his. This was a choice. This was a choice that I was making. The reasons for making it shriveled and turned to ash as I swam. Right here, right now. I was letting a person die. I'd never killed anyone before. I'd shot one person one time who was trying to kill me, but that woman had lived. This wasn't an attacker, Julia was innocent. She'd gotten caught in the machinations of something bigger and stronger than she was, and to save her son and my partner I chose to let her die. I was doing it without hesitation. I was doing it right now. My voice was screaming down a long, dark hallway, You don't need to do this. Go back. And I didn't. I kept going. I breathed air into the lungs of the boy with me. I fought growing exhaustion. I swam away from Julia Harris.

I don't know when she died.

I was nearly to shore when Joe began breathing on his own.

I laid him on the gravel beach. "Joe? Joe?" I asked, shaking him. Trying to get a response. There wasn't one. He kept coughing. That was encouraging. I rolled him over, laid him on his side. Let him spew forth briny bay water to make room for air. His breaths were desperate, and he still didn't wake up. The overcast sky did not give me nearly enough light. He was clammy to the touch and far too limp.

Every choice was dangerous now. Did I focus on Joe and risk allowing the vampire to surprise me? Do I focus on Peter and risk Joe's life? Joe's reedy breathing decided me. I didn't have the know-how to do more than watch. And when I reached for my cell phone to summon help, one press of a waterlogged button reminded me that it, too, had gone in the waters of Copano Bay. It was a large, beetle-black coaster.

Joe needed professional help now. To get that, I had to leave the kid on the beach, alone. Because I was going to have to go up to that pier, alone. And get to Peter, who I had to pray was not dead, and who would have, please god, a working cell phone. And if not him, one of the other people on the pier, but the logistics of calling help were less important than the glaring, obvious hurdle to getting there: Once I stepped foot on that dock, Camille was going to attack me too.

My inner organs were creosote. My throat had been scalded by the salt in the bay. I didn't have the speed or the weaponry to match a vampire's lethal capacity. My gun had also gone in the drink. It might fire wet, but "might" wasn't reassuring. I was essentially unarmed. But we were in daylight. She was sheltered by her blackout fabric and there were clouds still racing across the sky, but it was still pushing noon out here.

You're only rolled while the vampire is thinking about you. It's mind over matter, and this vampire showed she had the brain to win.

Maybe I could change her mind.

Chapter Ten

A half-dozen pickup trucks sat between me and the pier, all of them full of things I could use. Obviously I couldn't go get their owners' permission to raid them and it would be too much to hope for someone to leave a cell phone where I could get it—not with those big red parking signs saying Take your valuables with you. But I needed more tools than what I had. When a vampire is about to eat my partner, property ownership could bite me. I grabbed my water-logged gun, flipped it to the butt end, and slammed it into the nearest truck window. Safety glass shattered into small, bright pieces. There was a blanket on a seat and a cooler full of beer. Nothing more lethal. I grabbed the blanket and hurried over to Joe. Don't you die on me, kid. Next car. Shattered glass radiated out from my blow like diamond seeds. No dice. Car three, and I almost kicked myself for not looking through windows before I began shattering them. This guy had an impressive gun rack and the second down was a Remington. Thank you, God, for red-necks. I rummaged around in this unknown person's belongings and found the box of bird shot. If there hadn't been so many soft targets up on the pier, I would have taken the deer shot, but I was afraid of who Camille would use as a meat shield. I couldn't go for the kill.

And now to advance. Take the same path as before, only now running would be a mistake. Go slow. Take my time. Try to ignore the heart pumping needles of adrenaline rush. Ignore the fear. Use what cover I could. I pressed up against the admissions booth. The guy inside was blinking regularly. An encouraging sign. The vampire must be losing focus. Though that also raised the question: what could make a vampire strong-willed enough to roll the whole pier lose track of the plot? The answers made me scared for Peter and her other victims, and more determined than ever to act. I was going to stop this, and if Camille gave me a window, I was going to take it.

Step forward. Heart pounding. Could she hear that? Was I walking towards my own demise? Can't think about that. Step forward. And again.

I saw them. Nobody had died, but the vampire was practically melted into Peter. He stood unmoving, tears rolling down his face. Her cloth-shrouded face was close to his ear. The sun-obscuring cloak swirled around the body artfully, long and tight black pants showing the curve of leg and thigh.

I took a deep breath, burying the urge to jump out at the woman. I would get one shot. I needed to take out as much of her protection as possible. She was juggling twenty people or more; I needed to break her concentration. I got close. I couldn't make out her words, just the purring honey of her whispering to Peter. She shifted in her stance, one hand unwrapping the veil she'd placed around her head. As she did I braced myself and aimed for the head. Breathed deep…and that was a mistake. She heard me and her head snapped in my direction.

Fuck it all. Fire.

The shotgun sang a beautiful counterpoint to her soft, self-satisfied murmuring. Hundreds of pellets barely larger than sand hurled through the air. It wasn't going to be fatal, but it turned that big wheel hat into a lace doily, shredded her veil as if it were paper. Momentum and wind carried the now ruined cover into the bay. For one instant her beautiful face was exposed, her hair in a severe bun completely unlike her usual soft molten curls. She had no makeup on, but it was Camille. Then the cloud-shrouded sunlight began to eat into her features. That pearlescent skin, the eyes blue like sapphires, lips jewel red and full. All that poisoned loveliness began to burn.

Camille screamed, hands to her face. Steam rose between her clawed fingers. She snarled at me, fangs bared, but instead of attacking she wheeled around and leapt over the side of the pier. I reached for her, knowing how pointless that action was. She caught the rail and swung under the pier. Safe from the sun and out of my reach.

And as the hateful gothic apparition vanished into the cold darkness of the pier, Peter and the rest of her victims collapsed. She was safeguarding her escape, distracting me with the lives of her enthralled. And, goddamn her, it worked. To check on them, I had to let her go.

Peter first. He was awake, but had trouble responding correctly. Normal enough. Being rolled leaves the brain somewhat scrambled. I fished his phone out of his pocket and dialed 911 while I checked the next victim. And the next. Bob Harris looked to be unconscious, his broken fingers swollen and sausage-like. I moved his hand into a more stable position, the best I could do when I was soaked to the skin. When Peter sat up, I went back to him. Dispatch had hung up. "Help's on the way," I said, putting his phone in his pocket.

"What the fuck," he whispered.

And an engine coughed to life. Camille had apparently had a boat jammed under the pier. The same impulse shot through both of us, a dog's urge to chase. We hit the rail at the same time. Peter nearly went over into the drink. The small fishing boat arched away, the black shape, sans hat, at the helm.

"That was Camille Ward, Astrid. That was fucking Camille Ward." He said.

"I think we got that by now." And then my brain caught up with my adrenaline crash. "...the kid. I've got to go check on the kid." I said. I started to go.

"What about Julia?" Peter said.

I stopped. Fighting the urge to vomit, I said, "I couldn't...I couldn't get them both. She was unconscious by the time I got Joe to the surface, and...and I was afraid you all were going to die—"

"Jesus," Peter said, and pushed past me to go to the rail. He scanned the dark water for the secret unsurrendered. "Why didn't you say something sooner? What the fuck is wrong with you?"

I didn't answer. I couldn't. I ran back to the kid instead. My insides were a great black hole seconds away from singularity. Guilt was too neat of a word to encompass that, because it admits the idea of absolution. And the bigger sin was that I could not admit that feeling. I had to keep going.

We want morality to be easily sorted. Good guys. Bad guys. Clearly defined heroes who never fail and don't have flaws. Evil that comes without virtue. But this doesn't exist. We're all just people. We all either live up to expectations of basic morality, or we fail. And I had failed.

Joe was still breathing, but with a small hitch that I didn't like too much. Would he be okay until help got here? I didn't know what to do. His hands were ice cold. I was cold, too, my teeth chattering as I shivered. And I was afraid that if I took a minute, Joe wouldn't be alive when I came back.

And would it be help that came? I remembered the things Peter had said, earlier. Was it still today, that he'd said them? Just a few hours ago? It felt like another year, on another planet. He'd asked if I were seriously questioning why people liked Camille. I had always tried not to see a difference between people, between the magical and the mundane, between people like Joe and Peter and people like me. I'd always felt like that was the right way to do things. I'd never in my life ever called for help and been afraid that it would only make things worse. Now I was there, and the only thing I was sure of was that Peter had been here, maybe his whole entire life. Black apples are cats, I thought, and my shivers got worse.

I wish you could figure it out on your own. Had he said that because it was obvious? Because the only way to miss it was to be willfully blind?

I knew when they found her. The pitch of sounds behind me gained ragged desperation. Bob Harris screamed once. I didn't close my eyes but I couldn't look. Add that to the pile of failure and regret. I didn't want to see her come out of the water. I focused on Joe. His name was Joe. The Fae believe, with some justification, that names are power. Joe's name had to have power now. He was alive and he would, god help me, stay that way until help got here...if it was help.

Wasn't that a given, though? Wasn't that how the universe worked?

Of course not.

I felt so cold.

Joe breathed. I wanted to pick him up but didn't dare. I felt dirty. If I picked him up, wouldn't that dirt rub off? What if that killed him? I'd killed his mother. This was shock thinking, traumatized confusion, but I couldn't fight it. I could barely breathe. Why was it so cold? Footsteps crunched behind me. I spun around, too quick, too fast. I almost fell over. It was Peter, hands out as if comforting me. He'd gotten a blanket from somewhere. Probably one of the trucks I'd broken into. He gently lowered the blanket around my shoulders. Knelt down beside me. Lifted the boy into his strong arms. He took Joe's pulse, his face serious. "He breathing?"

I nodded. My teeth clicked together, a staccato underbeat against my heart.

"I shouldn't have said that," he said. "I'm sorry. You did what you could."

"She fought me. Camille made her fight me." I was shaking too hard to talk. Peter pulled me against him and began rubbing my shoulders. "What's going on up there?"

"Harris and a couple of the other people on the pier are trying to get her out. I told them to wait for a coast guard boat."

"I couldn't get them both, Pete. There wasn't any way for me to carry them both, I couldn't see, she was fighting me…" And anger. A small little spark. "You didn't have to let Camille roll you, Pete. You could have gone in there with me and we could have…I wouldn't have…We could have saved them both. I wouldn't have had to—"

Peter let go of me. "Astrid," He said, very softly. I finally met his eyes. They were very hard, filled with a rage I could not articulate. It wasn't aimed at me, because if it had been, it would have obliterated my existence. "I can't swim. I never got a chance to learn." He said.

Those words broke over me, ice cold and bleached by a pale lack of mercy. The sky above grew darker. Rumbles sounded far in the distance, coming nearer all the while. Peter didn't move from his vigil over the little boy. It was as if this were his child, as if he could protect the baby with his own body, be the shield he needed to survive the coming days. But Peter couldn't be that. I couldn't. His father couldn't. The boy was going to be cast on the mercy of a world whose machinations and cruelties had, in a way, been as responsible for his mother's death as Camille.

In a different world Peter might have known how to swim.

In the distance, the sirens sounded. Just before they reached us it began to rain.

Chapter Eleven

It took both me and Peter to keep the responding officers from handcuffing the little boy to the gurney. Peter stood at the center of three cops, his own credentials in hand, speaking in as calm and firm a voice as he possibly could. "Look at me. That kid did not kill Camille Ward. Camille Ward is the nearest thing to alive a vampire could possibly be. We have hard evidence. You ask anybody on that pier, they'll tell you they spent god knows how long under her—"

"You expect us to believe a vampire would roll a whole dock and not eat anybody?" One cop rolled his eyes.

"I saw it too. And I shot her goddamn hat off." I said. Too bad it wasn't her head.

"That kid needs to be in a hospital bed. He's four. And if he did kill anybody, it's because Camille rolled him same as she did his mom." Peter said. "He's her victim, not her killer."

71

"And how did you people botch body identification, if Ward is alive?" Asked the oldest of the cops. He seemed to be the one with the biggest chip on his shoulder.

"Because that's not how vampires work," I said. "We didn't have a body. A vampire is magic animating a corpse. You take that magic away and all you get is ash. We had a vacuum full of dust and a small, obscured camera across the street. It was her house and we didn't think there'd be two vampires in Corpus who would dress up like a fashion challenged balloon."

I heard a siren whoop. Bob Harris stood, forlorn, as the paramedics began closing the ambulance doors. Then, in a moment of mercy, they let him sneak into the back with his son. Doors closed. Engine starts. Now alive with energy, sound and lights, the ambulance roared off, down the road to the ER in Aransas Pass, thirty minutes away.

I thought somebody had said his eyes opened. I might have heard a small, plaintive voice asking for his mommy.

God. I just wanted to go to sleep.

"This is TA's jurisdiction, sir." Peter said. "I recommend you listen when somebody tells you something important."

"I know who I need to listen to," The cop said. "I'm going to recommend you two don't go too far."

I smiled real big at the guy. "Well, that's the good thing here: you know where we work."

Maggie called Peter's phone as we slowly drove back to Corpus. "Pete," He answered.

She said. "Fuck me. At least you two are alive. Did you get a piece of her before she bolted?"

"Yeah, but I don't think it was enough to slow her down." I said. "She got a flash burn from sunlight before she took off on a boat. I damaged her black-out suit but she can probably make cover if she tries." I said.

"Well, the bad news, before you ask, is that CCPD is rejecting my identification of these ashes. They want DNA verification, which they're not going to get." She said. "The boss is dialing activist groups to get that baby boy a lawyer. He should be okay. But…" she paused.

"But what, Mags?" Peter said.

"They're not going to go after her." She said.

"What? She just rolled twenty people and drowned a woman. Nearly killed a kid." I said. "Plus she killed her stand-in last night using Joe as a weapon. She's gone off the deep end—"

"And she's not going to stop. I hear you, Mija, and I said that and a whole lot more to the cops a few minutes ago." Maggie said.

"Lemme guess," Peter said, sounding even more tired. "They said even if she is still alive, her drowning a five-year-old boy could be viewed as self-defense."

"Yeah," Maggie said.

Peter began laughing, a nasty, bitter sound. "Never changes, you know? This shit. It never fucking changes. So what, we call the Hunters? Sic a lodge on her?"

There is still a formal order of vampire hunters. The Hunter Lodges, with their long historical lineage, are a staple of American roadway iconography; entering small towns you'd see their crossbow-and-knife symbol right next to the K of C seal. They dated back to medieval times. Terrestrial Affairs had mostly supplanted them, but the government kept them around. There were still things even we couldn't handle.

You can't kill a vampire without a warrant, and to get one you had to have a trial and conviction. The thing about Hunters, though, is they didn't always pay attention to those formalities. Sometimes it worked out in their favor. Sometimes it backfired and they had to surrender a few members or shutdown a lodge to avoid full-scale prosecution. Peter's willingness to let them stake Camille said all I needed to know about his mindset…and the fact that I agreed with him said a lot about mine.

After all, my ex-husband had been one of those Hunters.

"Can you be sure she couldn't talk her way out of the Lodge? She's been around a long time, Pete. You don't get this far with her track record if you don't have allies in high places."

Peter sighed.

"That said, you ready for the good news?" Maggie said. "I know why she's doing this."

I said. "Animal, vegetable or mineral?"

"Financial. Camille Ward has debt up to her fangs. Everything she owned is going back to the bank. Her cars, her house here, some properties she owns elsewhere. She's got maybe 50K in cash and based on what her financials look like, that was all going to her credit cards at the end of the month. Lady couldn't even buy her own blood."

"So how does faking her death help?" I asked.

"Well, you know how everybody pounced on this story? Her call records not only show that she never stopped using her cell, but that she's the one who made all the initial calls to the news desks. But before she did any of that? Hell, before I had a chance to vacuum up her stand-in? Something called the Camille Ward Legacy Foundation posted a campaign on a funding site. It talked about both the house here and her old plantation in Louisiana. Did you know it's up for sale?"

I whistled.

Peter said, "She's been invited back to that place multiple times."

"Not by the owners, she hasn't. Nobody has owned that place in full in over thirty years. There've been caretakers and even a board of directors, but no one person has had enough of a stake there to invite Camille permanently. Ownership is very important to vampires. They can't set foot on property without either a deed or an invitation. It's part of the magic keeping them alive. Camille lost that plantation. She didn't sell it. Her creditors were in the process of seizing it. She had to leave. That ownership transfer kicked her off her own land, she needed the permanent owner to invite her back in, and there hasn't been one in quite a while."

"That place hasn't sat empty for thirty years." Peter said.

"It isn't about legal authority. It's about magic and ownership. An invite from a board of directors isn't enough. She needs a singular owner, someone who has invested enough of themselves in the place that it's theirs. Between the multiple transfers between historical societies and the staff turnover when it was a museum, nobody fits the bill. Until that place sells, she can't go back"

"And now the same thing is happening with her house on Louisiana Avenue," I said.

"So, she's in debt, she's losing this house, and her old house is up for sale," Peter said.

"Lady's cashing in. How much is that campaign worth right now?" I asked.

"One point two million and rising." Maggie said. "And you read through the comments, it's about as thinly veiled as a weekend bedsheet washing at a diner named Karl's Kountry Kitchen. She's hitting racists up for money under the guise of saving the legacy of the Last Great Southern Belle."

"After being killed by a little Black boy," Peter said. I could hear volcanos burbling under his mild tone.

"Speaking of…boss's orders, Pete. You and Astrid need to come in."

The car got quiet. Peter's hands tightened on the steering wheel.

"She's obsessed with you, Pete, and the boss thinks she's desperate enough to throw out this second chance just to get to you. Boss used the phrase 'bunny boiler'. You need to get safe."

He didn't answer.

"Mijo, I'm gonna say this. I'm gonna say this once. You get your ass down here and go into protective custody. I don't care what you say," And she overrode Peter's protest. "I don't trust her any further than I could stake her. I want your ass here, under guard, until that woman is ash in a garbage bag. You copy?"

"Sure," Peter said, calmly. Way too calmly. And he remained just as calm as he ended the call.

My sense for Peter's private Earthquake country hadn't abated one iota. "We're not going to HQ, are we?"

"We're not going to HQ." He said.

"You know where she is?" I asked.

"I know where she told me she'd be," He said.

There weren't a whole lot of places a vampire could hide. And only one of them that Camille would feel worthy of her greatness. "You don't have to do this." I said. "You don't have to go to her house. You can just let everybody else do their job."

"Will they?" Peter said, quietly.

We drove on in silence for a few minutes, passing through Rockport at a sedate, legal speed. "What did she say to you on the pier?" I said.

"How well she knew my granddad. She said that she made it a point to know all her slaves' names." And though he seemed calm on the outside, the engine gunned and our speed increased.

There was more to it than that. There had to be. She'd cut him deep. It was strange, being on the outside of someone else's story. Was his pain one of those things I wasn't supposed to know? But I thought, too, about the times I'd been hurt. How I winnowed through my own thoughts and history, choosing what others should know. And so I let it go.

"So what should we do?" I said.

"You're not asking me that, Astrid. You're trying to talk me out of what we should do," he said, and changed lanes. "Tell me I'm wrong, but there was a minute were you were afraid to get that kid to a hospital. Because you didn't know what was going to happen next."

I was suddenly fighting the urge to vomit. I could feel that dark water around me once more. I said, "You're not wrong."

"Do you really believe anybody is ever going to punish Camille Ward?"

My fingers, prying Julia Harris's hands off her son. "No. But…does it have to be you?" I said.

Silence again. We were out of Rockport, driving down a sparse road now surrounded by wetlands, heading towards Aransas Pass. Everything was browning and dying, the water drying up. Cattails lined the ditches to either side of the road, a vibrant trace in the dreariness of this horrible autumn day. And still everything seemed so gray.

"When was the first time you saw her name? I'm always curious, you know. When do normal…" he stopped. Checking himself. Committing. "When do white people start noticing this stuff? When was the first time you knew she existed?"

"I…don't know. I think it was on a movie channel. They showed the movie about her cousin, the one she had a part in. The movie channel made a big deal about having Sally Ward's actual relative in the picture." They'd even shown that famous photo. Camille, with the blood and the champagne flute.

"And they said it like it was a good thing." He shook his head. "Do you know the first time I saw her name? It was on a bill of sale for my great grandfather. My gran was doing genealogy, and Camille's plantation uploaded its archives, and there was her signature. Like, I don't know, he was a bag of sugar or something." He gave me a look, one that appeared to question the value of every cell in my body, then said very slowly, "Camille owned my great-grandfather."

Well. That explained the obsession with Peter. But he wasn't done talking.

"Back at HQ, when I hit Max, he was asking about the difference between Camille and the men they killed up North. And I bet you don't get it either. Oh, you see that something wrong happened, but you don't get it. It took a miscarriage of justice, murder, police corruption and goddamn riots to get you people to notice. Camille faked her death and framed a child for it, and now she gets what she wants. She's famous. She's an icon. She targeted that kid like he was a gazelle on the veldt. The woman makes murder into glamour shots. And everybody loves her."

I think Peter wanted to stop there, but he couldn't. He was caught in release. The words spilled out like blood.

"My parents died when I was eleven. It was an accident. It was horrible. Nobody cared. My grandmother died when I was sixteen. Some dumb white kid in a Jag smashed into her when he sped through a light. He was drunk. He got…I think it was a couple years' probation and a suspended license. They blamed affluenza. Like wealth is something contagious. I never even had a chance to know granddad. He had a heart attack. They made him wait twelve hours in the ER, until he collapsed in the waiting room. He was dead before they got him onto the gurney.

"I don't know where I came from, past her. You know why that shit about a red-haired sorcerer pisses me off? Because…because maybe it's true. And maybe if I'd been born with people who knew what to look for, maybe my…" He stopped. Swallowed. "Maybe my life would be different. But I don't get to know that. It's just gone. No. It's not gone. It's taken. Taken by people like her and people like Max and people like…like…" He stopped.

"Like me," I said.

He paused for a moment, caught in a habitual collection of apology, and then said nothing. It was a deliberate silence. An agreeable one.

"I'm sorry," I said.

"You're sorry," Peter said, nodding to himself. "Astrid, you don't even know what you're apologizing for."

Silence, as we drove through the back roads of South Texas. These were the places where secrets got buried. I watched the wetlands pass by because I had nothing to say.

He sighed. "You're not the good guy in this story. You're not the bad guy either, but…" he stopped and rubbed his eyes. Clenched his hands tighter on the wheel. "Who else is going to do it? How long do we have to let her keep doing this? She's a stain on the fucking world."

I knew that. You only had to read about her victims to know she was a monster beyond the pale. "I'm just not used to breaking the rules on this scale." I said.

"I can let you out. You can go tell Maggie and the boss that I'm going to go confront Camille. I'm pretty sure you could even find somebody in the organization who would give you a cookie," He said. "You know. For saving one of the last living pieces of the Confederacy."

"It might even make Max Arrows like me," I said, and tried to smile. It didn't work. I kept feeling cold water pressing into the back of my throat. It tasted like blood. I was so incredibly tired. "Alright. I'm with you. Let's go kill a vampire."

Chapter Twelve

Camille Ward's house was blocked off with crime scene tape. Ends fluttered in the afternoon breeze. Her perfect lawn had been destroyed by tire tracks. A vengeful little part of me hoped she had noticed. It was still overcast, but the storm in Rockport didn't reach this far. There were glimpses of blue through the clouds. Enough sunlight that even with the oaks and that magnolia tree, her yard was impassable. She'd be contained if she didn't have that black-out suit on.

We were back on Louisiana Avenue. Full circle.

"How you want to do this?" I said.

"Let her take me, and then you take her." He said.

I nodded. "So just like on the pier?"

"Just like on the pier." Peter said.

He was scared, drenched in sweat, and his hands trembled as he secured his identification and gun. Moon Silver jewelry on, not that it had done us much good so far. He swallowed compulsively. Holstered his piece. Glared up at the house, which seemed to loom back over us.

"She could roll us both," I said.

"Yep." He said. "You really don't have to go in with me."

"Really? We're going to do this again?" I said. The last time we'd had this conversation, I'd been joking. Peter hadn't. Not that time. Not this time, either. "I've got your back. As long as you're willing to have me."

He grabbed my shoulder and squeezed it. Contact. Acknowledgement. We weren't two ships passing in the dark, we were together on the boat ride to hell. There to the end.

Her door was ajar again. Wasn't that the punchline for a bad joke? This time the entry lights were on, exposing a floor that was clean. Too clean. Maggie hadn't mopped it, and if she had, she would have used lavender Fabuloso. This floor smelled of bleach and lemon.

SOP exists so you know what to do when fear gnaws at your gut. Our training said to clear the ground floor first, then go upstairs. Left turn from the front door went to a sitting room, the nearest thing to an old-fashioned parlor you'd find outside of a museum. The last time we had seen this place it was spartan and being tidied by Camille's housekeeper. Today, it was empty of people and filled with stuff, a dragon's hoard of silk and shiny things. There was just enough room to walk between the tables of tiny enamel boxes, the display cases of antique hand-fans. A baby grand piano had been crammed into one corner, topped by a stained glass lamp that I hoped wasn't a genuine Tiffany. Around the lamp's iron feet, a swath of fur stole draped around knickknacks and memorabilia. Old flowers in a shadowbox. Empty perfume bottles. The newest addition was display case of African objects, each one with a small cardboard label as if this were a museum, mixed with an ominous selection of iron implements. The only one I recognized were a pair of handcuffs. But Peter's jaw became very set, the lines of his face even harder than before.

The room behind the parlor could have been a TV room or a dining nook, if you cleared the piles of belongings out of it. But it was full, floor to ceiling, with stuff. Peter and I exchanged a look.

We found a body in the kitchen. An older man, ruggedly handsome and very white. This was both his race and the result of bloodletting; his throat had been slit. She'd made him strip before she killed him, and his clothes and ID were gone. She'd posed his body in the sink as if he were a turkey, placed a half-rotten apple in his mouth. I couldn't react beyond the initial lurch in my gut. Peter threw the apple into the bin, picked the man up and laid him down on the kitchen floor. I pulled a shawl out of Camille's great wall of stuff. It was wider and longer than it ought to have been, felt expensive. I laid it on the body. The blood soaked in.

There was a punchbowl of blood and a glass to one side, garnished with red oranges and mint. A small card sat in front of this, with the word Peter in perfect copperplate calligraphy. I could hear her voice, irritated by having to get her rabies shots. I'm not a (pardon the word) damn dog to need a (pardon) damn dog tag.

Even dogs are honest with their kills.

There were two bedrooms on the ground floor. One had been set up as a writing room. Not what we would think of as a modern office, though there was a slimline laptop shoved under a stack of foolscap. The rolltop desk was packed full of paper and calligraphy pens. Camille wrote her own letters. But the tell was the stack of old-school Hollywood headshots still in a box, all of them well-aged and some of them pre-signed. I remembered a clip from Mommie Dearest, Joan Crawford autographing pictures for her fans. I wondered if Camille had fantasized about that when she got a role in her cousin's biopic. Having her own beautiful image fifty feet high on the silver screen. Soirees and expensive champagne served magnanimously and handsome young men fighting over a chance to lie on her bed and donate to her multiple appetites. Fame. She'd watched it dwindle away, too, going out like the life from a strangled lover.

Except she still had a fan list, if the addressed envelopes were anything to go by. Most of the names I recognized as southern politicians. Some of them I knew from periodic checks of the FBI's Most Wanted list. She was playing games with other predators. The Last Great Southern Belle knew her audience, alright.

The last room was a guest bedroom that smelled of mothballs. I doubted anyone had ever slept in that bed. It was a Potemkin village with frilly lace curtains and television five years out of date. As if she ever intended to have a human guest stay there and survive.

Time to go upstairs.

She'd left a door open down at the end of the hall, had placed candles and rose petals on the floor. However the next few minutes were going to go, Camille was making the best of it. This was her stage, her show.

"Clear the rest of the house," Peter muttered. I nodded and went to the first closed bedroom door.

It was her closet, packed full of beautiful things. The wide crinoline petticoats and whale-bone corsets, some made of silk so old it was held together by memory and thought, some so new that the polyester tags were visible. The dresses. Yard after yard of jewel tone silk, velvet and tulle. Hand made lace collars and cuffs, embroidered and beaded shawls strung from ceiling to door jam. Shoes dating from every fashion period, each in their own lined cubby. This was where Camille's withered heart existed most clearly, here in the place where she built her façade.

And then in the next room, we found the real Camille.

Every wall was covered in historical papers. Photographs of Black men and Black women in neat lines and ragged clothes. Reproductions of daguerreotypes, men with sun-battered faces and hopeless eyes staring into the camera. A woman in a calico gown holding up a white child to the camera, the baby in an elaborately made christening dress. These photos, this woman, this baby, progressed until the Black woman was old and the child was visibly Camille. And then there was one photo of a pair of boys. Sixteen, maybe. Their clothes were shredded into rags and nearly nothing, but they were different from the other photographs. These men were still defiant. I fixated on one of them, because his chin was square to the camera, his eyes hard and angry, his fists clenched.

Peter tapped it. "My great-granddad. He and another kid tried to escape and…" he trailed off.

On the opposing wall, there was a second reproduction of that same picture. Only it was surrounded by newer, more modern photos. Genealogy print outs. Stories about families, lists of names scratched out. Newspaper clippings—Family home burns down; boy only survivor—with a boy who would, clearly, grow into Peter Jennings. And on the other side, photos of Bob Harris and his little boy. If you followed the genealogies you'd find one defiant one in Peter's family, and the other one, the ancestor of Bob Harris.

None of it had been random. Not even Joe.

But then, that fit, didn't it? She didn't want any house, she wanted her old plantation. Vampires need minions the same way they need housing. Camille was looking for what she felt was hers. Her house. Her stuff. Her slaves. If you looked at the world through heartless eyes, everything she had done made sense.

Peter took a few deep breaths. Tears ran down his cheeks, leaving blue-black trails on his skin. "Fuck her," He whispered. "Come on."

We didn't look into any other room. We walked together, shoulder to shoulder, straight into the lair of the dragoness herself. Peter lead. I followed.

Right before his hand touched the door, she trilled, in a voice that was pure sugar and honey, "Enter, darlin'. And leave some of the happiness you bring."

We entered.

Chapter Thirteen

Camille Ward was nearly naked. She had dressed in a modern negligee, black tulle embroidered with white magnolias, a modified a La Perla number. Beneath it, black bra and thong. The flat landscape of her belly gleamed as ivory under the silk, and her breasts rose from the foamy neckline lace like some polished lunar binary, glowing without crater or flaw. Candles had been set around her bed. They gleamed off her shoulders, brought golden light to the pale curls of her hair. She looked like an X-rated fairy princess. Except half her face was covered by an artful sweep of tress and that still was not enough to hide the deep burns. Sunlight had eaten through dermis, and possibly deeper. Boat is slower than car. She hadn't had long to prepare for display. Set up her candles. Choose her clothes. Lay herself out like a buffet.

For Peter.

She lay on a bed covered in silk. Not just sheets but scarves and lacy throws. Her instinct for stuff, ever-more stuff, had extended even to here. She surrounded herself with roses and silk, and more blackout curtains, topped by heavy brocade set into tracts that bordered every wall.

There was something pathetic about it, something difficult to articulate. Maybe it was just how hard she was trying. Desperation has a scent. She stank of it. Performative sexuality stripped of anything that would give it meaning or value, existing just to shock.

With one smooth arm, she lifted her champagne glass of blood. Cut crystal. Only the best for the bloodsucker. She swirled it, as if she were appraising the contents.

"I'm disappointed you didn't want any of the libations downstairs. It's so hard to find a good O-neg donor on short notice. You're gonna learn, those are the best. Rare is its own kind of sweet." She said and took a sip from her glass. She tilted it a bit too far, deliberately, so that the blood dripped from the corners of her mouth. It rolled down her chin, her throat, her cleavage. She met Peter's eyes and I thought this is it, here we go, but she didn't roll him. Instead, she wiped the blood up with her fingers, a display of sensuosity that ended with her red manicured nails vanishing into her mouth as she sucked the blood off her fingertips.

"See anything you like?" She said.

"No," Peter said, and didn't add that unless she suddenly developed a pulse and started identifying as a dude he never would.

"You will. But I wanted us to talk. And…just…us."

She pulled a small remote control out from under a silken pillow and pushed a button. The curtains that bordered the room withdrew, exposing mirrors. Hundreds of them, from small wall mounted ones barely large enough for a face to multi-pane full length monsters ripped straight from a department store. They were on the walls, on the ceiling, even a couple angled on the floor. And the safe space I had chosen to look at was now reflecting her face. Every single mirror on the walls had been angled so that she could tilt her head and have her image reflect in a thousand different windows. She was reflecting. Vampires aren't supposed to do that.

"Did you know? We can reflect in a Moon Silver mirror." And she paused for us to appreciate just how much money was glimmering and shimmering on the walls around us. How much she had shelled out just for the image of her own face. She didn't need to do all this to get her house back. All she'd need to do is sell a few of these. Give up her obsession with her own face. "And we can do a lot more than just look pretty." And in the mirror, she met my eyes.

It happened like an impact. One moment my body was mine. The next, it wasn't. Every cell, every tissue, every sinew now obeyed her. I breathed with her permission. My heart beat with her say-so. And whatever plan Peter had before, it was now effectively dirt. I could not even clench my fists in anger.

"That's better. Most people don't know about the mirror trick. It's useful when your pets know better than to make eye contact. Oh, Peter, did you think I'd let you bring backup? She isn't pretty enough to be our third wheel."

Peter dropped his head, eyes to the unmirrored floor. Transfixed and immobile, I could still watch them in the mirrors. That was all I could do. I was worse than useless meat. I was a hostage. "I came here to arrest you for killing Julia Harris. Let her go and--"

"You can't arrest shit." Anger and offence shredded her beauty for a moment. But she stilled herself, doused the venom in honey. "You're not a cop. And even if you were, even if you did, I've got friends in high places. It always pays to keep powerful friends. You haven't learned that yet. You'd waste your time on your silly nurse and her little Black boy, when you could have me." She clucked her tongue. "But you were always going to come here. It's what you're destined for."

Peter did not look at her, but I could read his outrage in every stiff line of his body. "What?"

She stood up, pacing towards him with feline grace. "I am the reason you are alive. I am the reason your great-grandfather lived to reproduce. I am the reason your parents existed to make you. You owe me everything. And I am here to collect." She rocked forward, tilting her head sweetly…and trying, I think, to make eye contact with Peter. "Don't worry. It's confusing to be human, I understand. You've been lead wrongly. But one day you're gonna see I'm right." She had walked nearly all the way around him, and he'd kept her out of his gaze, tracking her more by sound than sight. "I'm tired of living in shadows. Letting some upstart mulatto in Houston tell me what to do? Please. I'm making my play. I'm gonna be Master in this town. And you're going to be my right hand. They stole you. I'm stealing you back."

"Stealing me from what? Myself?" Peter said

"Don't play stupid," And she leaned in close, intimate, those ruby lips nearly brushing his ear. "I told you on the pier, I know what you are." She withdrew just a bit, waiting for his response. He didn't give her one. Some of her gloating pleasure died as she watched his non-reaction. Her lip curled, contempt through her mask. "I see your heritage in you. Everything you are, everything that waits within you, all of it is mine." She breathed the last like something from a porn movie, her breasts heaving. It took work to do that, especially when you had so much to work with. "Don't you see how we're not that different? We've both lost everything, over and over again. They keep on coming and taking it away from us. My home is there, it's waiting for me. And it's your home too. Your ancestor's blood is there. They're buried on my land. This is my chance to get it back. And I'm going to bring you with me."

"I'd say you're not right, but you know what? That sounds about white to me," He said, eyes still on the floor. "And you're right, I don't have the power to arrest you. But if you turn yourself in, I'll keep you alive until the trial."

She didn't see what he was doing. The way his body tensed, the way he kept her at a specific spot in his field of view. I'd seen him do this before in the sparring ring and it made my gut clench. He was getting ready for something.

"Forget the posturing. Forget the rules out there. This is what matters. I am what matters. I want to see your strength, Peter." And then she bent even nearer, until she was almost touching him. "I want to see your fire."

"Last chance, Camille." His left hand reached back, where I knew he kept his gun.

"Alright, my love. Let's raise the stakes." And she raised her hand. Pointed at me, while still looking at him, and said "Don't breathe."

And my lungs stopped working.

My body responded as if it were already oxygen starved. It remembered the bay, the dark water closing in while I struggled with Joe Harris in my arms. The burn hadn't started, but it was going to come. It creeped up on me like some leonine thing, purring as my body used what air it had. My muscles wanted to breathe. My brain commanded them to. The pain of my body's disobedience was something that they'd left out of the literature. Being rolled hurt. And the air wasn't coming. My body screamed, why not? Peter stared in horror, forgetting about Camille for one split second. His plan had been for me to save him. And as he stared, she moved like a lightning strike, stole the gun from his belt and threw it into a corner.

"Humans are such small, weak things. You crush beneath me like red cherries. And you taste just as sweet. Submit to me or she dies," Camille said.

No, Peter. Don't do it. Don't do what she wants. Or do what she wants and save me because the burn is starting. It's turning me to ash one tissue at a time. Save yourself. Save me. Altruism and biology warring out inside of me and it still served no point because I could do nothing. Camille owned me in ways I hadn't imagined possible. And she knew it. The agony in my lungs was equaled only by the exquisite pain of her grip on my body. And oh god I just wanted to breathe.

Peter turned away from me. Not looking at her. Not looking at me. My life was in his hands. And he could leave me. He could run from here like I had left Julia Harris. I had not earned his rescue, I had not become something worthy of his friendship. And the part of me not consumed with a growing hunger for air said yes, good, please go. Save yourself.

But that wasn't who he was.

"You want my fucking fire?" He said, and with those words her face turned exalted. But he still did not look at her. "Fine. Take it."

And then he moved. For all our jokes about Ichabod Crane, there was speed and grace in those long legs. It exploded out of him with purpose and power. He wheeled like a falcon; he danced. He grabbed the nearest candle and threw it, but not at her. She'd recoiled because that was what she expected. An attack on her sacred person. But he nailed the mass of blackout curtains covering the windows. The candle seemed to burst with hot wax and flame. The curtain went up with a woosh.

With the same motion, he kicked out the nearest mirror. It shattered into long fragments. He grabbed the largest, two pieces of silvered glass nearly as long as his forearms. Her face was reflected back at her. In her haste she'd bared her burns. Her cheekbone was visible through the deep wounds on her cheek, as were a few of her pearlescent teeth. The ruin of her left eye dripped fluid, its socket twitching around the damaged optical nerve. Peter's chosen weapon was not safe. The sharp edges ate into his hands. His blood flowed. It dripped off his wrists onto the floor. But it was shed by his choice, for his fight. Bleeding was an act of defiance.

"Why would you do that?" She shrieked. Wrath and fear had transformed her face. The beauty was gone, drained into the strident lines of shrieking. "You're going to kill us, you little shit!"

"Long as you go first," he said, and came at her.

She was faster than him, stronger than him, but she wasn't a fighter. Pete was. Her movements were predictable and as Peter learned her pattern, he began to cut her. Dodge, and his makeshift knife slashed down the front of her negligee, near her heart. A feint and he cut her across her burned cheek. Each time she came forward or dodged an attack, Peter anticipated her movement. Brought the glass to where she would be, forced her to rethink. She pulled her movements before he could connect lethally, but she was getting hurt faster than she could heal.

She hadn't forgotten about me. I still couldn't breathe. Now it was agony, a vice around my lungs. The fight and the fire both slid away like melting butter. The roar in my ears was not flame; it was suffocation. I was going to die here because I hadn't been quick enough to look away from Camille's eyes. I cast around inside myself for some kind of positive thought and the only one that came was at least now you know what Julia Harris went through.

And then her grip ebbed. I could inhale. Not by much, but the thin thread of oxygen tore through my lungs. It felt like a knife down my throat. My head cleared, just a bit. I could almost move on my own.

Camille held her arm. Fluids from blood that had long ago separated pattered down onto the ground. Vampires bleed, they just bleed dead. Peter rolled back into an observational stance, his own blood saturating his shirt sleeves. The flesh on his palms was starting to resemble hamburger, but he wasn't letting go of the mirror fragments. Camille's own face stared back from his weapons. Her hair was singed off in places now, her ruined skin sallow. She snarled, baring fangs, and tried to get around the glass to Peter's throat. If she weren't telegraphing her moves so obviously, he would have been dead. Instead, he stepped aside at the right moment and tore his glass down her back, shredding furrows into her dead skin.

The fire had spread to another set of curtains, was pooling against the ceiling, racing across popcorn nubs to the fan. One of the supporting rings of the curtain gave out, allowing the first rays of sunlight into the room. The smoke and the heat was now as great a threat as Camille's will. I could not move well enough to escape, and with the fire devouring the air, I was getting dizzier by the second.

Peter fought on. Camille had figured out she couldn't get to him by rushing. She used her precious belongings to keep him at bay. The vanity table. A plaster bust of herself. A jewelry box filled with costume jewelry. The bits of glass and faux gold sparkled when she broke it over Peter's head. And he was resolute. Implacable. He deflected each blow with a masterful precision. He used her wealth to shatter her mirrors. Each precious object in her hoard shattered yet another one of her images. It gave Peter more room, more places where he could not be ensnared. And with that freedom, he did real damage. The lovely La Perla negligee hung in shreds. The wounds he carved into her former perfection gaped like fault lines in the earth. It exposed the dead nature of her body, the monstrosity beneath the façade. She was a cadaverous ruin spewing rotten blood. But he was starting to falter. One of her many boxes hit his shoulder with a bone-aching sound. The fire and the heat were undoing him, bit by bit.

Her attention had slipped enough that I could move and breathe freely. Or maybe she had let go, recognizing that it didn't matter. The fire was killing me. I sank to my knees in a pile of paper ashes and broken glass, my thought fraying and sleep, sweet and perfect and lethal, sleep was pulling me down. I stared into my own face, replicated a thousand times by Camille's mirrors.

We were going to lose if something didn't change.

The curtains were still burning.

I had to help Peter. I had to make one right decision.

The curtains.

I couldn't throw a punch. I was no match for Camille. But I could still do one thing, couldn't I? I could clear the air.

I staggered forward, and as I reached the burning curtains I knew my initial plan wasn't going to work. I didn't even have the strength to tear them down.

Peter coughed. He hadn't dropped his makeshift weapons, but that moment was getting close. Smoke obscured more than fire revealed. Peter was losing the advantage due to simple biology: Camille was dead. She could burn, probably would burn, but not before our need to breathe killed us both. And Camille crouched in an unburning corner, licking her ruby red lips and waiting. She'd figured it out. She could afford to wait.

"Pete," I said, calling his attention to me. To what I was about to do. He saw me. His eyes narrowed just a bit. The roar of fire echoed around us. His eyes tracked to the curtains, and then back to me. I nodded, once, and watched as he accepted it. We'd worked together a long time.

I was going to give him another chance to take her out.

I threw myself at the windows. With every ounce of strength I had left I flung myself into the burning curtains…and into the glass behind them.

Windows aren't made for that kind of weight. This one popped out of the frame. There was a burst of explosive fire behind me as fresh oxygen fueled the flashover. I spilled through the afternoon air, tumbling down in a cloud of burning fabric and glass, down until I hit the earth. The impact of Camille's manicured lawn knocked what little air I still had out of my lungs, and when I rolled out from beneath the windows I sliced myself badly on the outer thigh. But there was air here and the flaming curtains burned themselves out on the damp lawn. I laid on the grass and stared up.

Peter leapt from the window with panther-pawed grace, aiming for the magnolia tree just off to one side. Smarter than me. He caught a branch, gripped it hard. Blood from his hands splattered on the tree. I had no idea how he could grip when his palms were hamburger. But magnolia trees aren't known for their strength. The branch snapped off in his hands, as did the next. His weight and desperation stripped most of the branches off of the house side of the tree. When he landed, it was on a cushion of magnolia flowers and branches, completely obliterating the zinnia bed beneath.

He didn't linger on impact, either, but rolled onto his hands and knees. He was ready for the second round. He knew that there would be one. But somewhere in all of that, he'd dropped his mirror shards. He had no weapon.

With a woosh and perfect poise, Camille landed in the grass between him and me, in a pool of shadow from her house. She had partial protection from the sun. It wasn't enough to protect her for long. Soon she'd have a set of full body burns to match the destruction of that pretty face. Steam already rose from her shoulders and thighs. But she'd have enough time to damage us before she had to stop. And all I could do was roll over onto my side and moan in agony. I was pretty sure I'd broken something. And the fire billowed out of the room above us all, a portal into hell.

Camille walked towards Peter, her feet dainty and steaming in the shadow-dappled grass. "You know," she said. "Maybe you aren't worth it. All that time. All that sacrifice. And all I've got is a dirty little—"

Peter stood in one smooth motion, his back still to Camille. "Shut up."

"Don't you tell me to shut up, boy. Do you know what I've lost! What I spent for you!" She shouted.

"I don't give a fuck what an ugly monster like you thought you get. Shut. Up."

With a scream of rage, Camille launched herself at Peter. Her skin snaped and popped like frying chicharrons as she passed through sunlight beams. He kept his back to her until the last second, turning only in the heartbeat before their bodies met. Where someone else might show fright, Peter was unyielding. He invited her in that moment, his arms even moving to receive her. There was green in his hands as they came up. And just before they met, he closed his eyes.

She slammed into Peter, her face buried in the curve of his throat. There was a horrible, meaty sound, something tearing and bleeding. And I screamed too because I couldn't get up. I couldn't do anything. My friend was going to die and I couldn't save him.

There was a sound like a small animal crying. And Camille backed away from Peter.

No. She staggered, her hands suddenly gathered at her chest, and she was the one making those sounds, those small, hurting animal sounds. Peter's expression was a grim mask of stone. Only his eyes had emotion and they burned. He was almost aflame with hate and disgust…and triumph.

She faced me, spasming as her body short-circuited. I had been wrong. Peter had been armed the whole time. A magnolia branch impaled the middle of her chest. He had used her momentum to drive it home.

It wasn't an instant death. He must have barely nicked her heart. It was enough to undo the magic that kept her living, but slowly. Like a marionette puppet with her strings cut, she dropped into the grass on her knees. Her mouth and hands both worked with the pointless noise of an engine grinding down. She fell onto her back gracelessly. Her head made a rotten sort of hollow sound when it hit the earth. unlight ate into one bare shoulder, dissolved a large chunk in the side of her thigh. She looked up at Peter and reached for him, an expression of longing on her face.

And Peter, without mercy, crossed the lawn to the broken panes of glass. He hefted up the largest.

"Save me," She whispered, though nothing could save her now. Her hand slid slowly to the ground as the sun burned her strength away. "Love me." She said. Her head turned back and forth as her eyes unfocused. "Tell me I'm—"

Peter's piece of glass had an edge like a guillotine. He drove it into her throat. Fresh blood spurted from the deep cuts in his hands. None of it fell on the vampire. Her head spun away and whatever last words she had perished as her burned and ruined face tumbled into a puddle of sunlight.

"I'd say go to hell," Peter whispered, over her dissolving body. "But you're not even worth the devil's time."

Chapter Fourteen

It was late on Friday when they came for Camille's ashes. Her real ones. Certified by at least two magical practitioners, of whom Maggie was one. She was, without a doubt, comprehensively dead. The estate from Kentucky even brought a small, jeweled box to put them in. There was a press conference and the promised rally. I didn't know Corpus Christi even had Confederate reenactors, but they arrived in gray wool uniforms, waving the Confederate flag and looking an especially purple shade of miserable. It might be November, but the heat radiating off the asphalt made their period-perfect wool coats shimmer. They talked about the death of the Last Great Southern Belle. Tears rolled down faces powdered with various shades of ivory and ecru, speeches about the glories of old were given. The stars and bars waved overhead, and the fake uniforms glittered, and people stood proud and united under Camille's famous photo, her drinking a cup of her victim's blood. The image was stapled to dowel rods and printed on t-shirts. They wanted to remember that. Even that.

No one talked about Julia Harris, or Joe, or Bob, or any of the thousands of people she had murdered both before and after her turning. I'm sure that if the true scope of her machinations hadn't come out, they would have been mentioned in negative terms as thinly veiled calls to action. But now that they were victims, they got swept under the crinolines to be forgotten with all the rest. Instead of mentioning her murders, her appetite, the violence she had visited on this part of Texas, they spoke of her beauty and her place in history. Someone talked about financial reforms so that the remnants of a greater time would never have to be so desperate again. Someone else quoted Gone with the Wind.

It all tasted like ashes.

Peter watched it all, standing beside me. He waited until the pretty, sparkly box was placed in the safety of an expensive rental car. Then he turned away and walked down the beachfront. It was a long, straight shot from the American Bank Center, curving past hotels and expensive condos, terminating at Cole Park right in front of Louisiana Street. He didn't go that far. Neither of us had any desire to revisit a monster's burned out home. The stretch from the Bank Center to the T-head docks was lined by a whitewashed railing, interrupted now and then by the concrete Miradores Del Mar gazebos. There was only one that was different; it had been repurposed into a memorial for Selena Quintanilla-Perez, a famous Tejano singer who had been murdered by a fan. Peter stopped there, just past her statue, walked to the rail overlooking the water, and stood still. He kept his poor, ruined hands in his pockets and said nothing. Scowling. Thinking. Hurting.

I waited beside him.

"You know what the second most common way for women to die back then was?" Peter said. He watched the water a few more minutes. "Fire. The big skirts kept knocking over candles and falling into fireplaces."

"Or they got blown away. Caught under a wagon wheel," I said. "Thrown into water. Drowned." I bit my lip for a second. "They're not even mourning her, are they?"

"Not the her we saw. But she was always a fucking vampire. It was just a lateral move when she got turned." He said. "And because they don't see her, she still got what she wanted. She's finally on her way home."

I sighed, because this could really get me into trouble. Then I took a bag out of my pocket and handed it to him. "Here."

The ash in it was fine and even. Getting my barbeque ash to match had been a bear. I'd been up half the night picking unburned charcoal chunks out of my coffee grinder. But it was worth it to make the switch. Peter did not touch it. "What is that?" He said, though he probably already knew.

We all know the look of dead vampires.

I glanced around. "Don't you mean, who?"

He stared at me.

"The Ward estate is going back to Kentucky with the charcoal ash from that batch of ribs we ate the last time you came for a barbeque. She's not going home."

He still didn't take the bag. "Why?" He said.

"Because she wanted to die. That's what this was. She didn't have enough time to get the money for her plantation. As far as anyone can tell, she didn't have a new identity lined up. She couldn't stand the idea of diminishing, so she decided to die. All of this was just her suicide attempt. She wanted to end things on her own terms." I shook the bag. "I figured you'd want to change the terms."

He continued to stare at the bag. I felt anxious. As if maybe this hadn't been the right gesture to make. And it probably hadn't been. Putting my foot in it was my own special gift.

"Look," I said. "I'm…starting to figure things out. I see your point from the other day. How I need to work this sort of thing out. I don't know the right answer—"

"That's on you," Peter said. He took a deep breath and sighed. "I'm sorry. But it has to be. I don't want Camille to be what defines my life. I never want to see that fucking flag ever again. I never want talk about Gone With the Wind like it's about something. I want this to be the smallest chapter in my story, and I can't get that if I have to spend my time explaining why to white people. I know how bright you are, Astrid. I know you can work this out if you try, and I have to ask you to try. I don't have enough of me to give to every bloodsucker who wants it. I have to take care of me first. I love ya, Astrid. You're one of the better white friends I've ever had. But I don't owe you anything."

"And I'm telling you…" I stopped. Took a deep breath. "I'm promising you that I'm going to learn. I am going to try. And…well…Camille." I shook the bag. "This was the only thing I could think to do."

"There is a difference," Peter said, "Between 'trying' and handing me a dead vampire in your lunch bag."

I grinned, involuntarily. You could even see the mustard stains. "I made sure you were on camera somewhere else when I made the switch. If they ever figure it out, I'm on the hook. Not you."

His hands had something of a tremble as he took Camille's ashes. I'd used a sandwich bag for the switch. I hadn't been entirely careful to make sure it was a clean one. Part of the Last Great Southern Belle clung to the mustard stain from my sandwich.

He said, softly. "It's not enough. But…it works." Pause. "Thank you."

"Okay," I said.

"It's not okay," he said.

"I'm learning that," I said.

And then there was that twinkle, that spark of the Peter that wasn't overwhelmed by the choices other people had made. His long, graceful fingers danced, wing-like, over the bag. I saw his own choice flare in his eyes, a moment of pyroclastic genesis. "Stay here, Astrid. I gotta go make a deposit." He said.

There were a set of public restrooms further up on the T-head. Not all the boats had bathrooms, and not everybody on the t-heads had a boat. I could smell the things from here. Peter, fastidious, opened the door with his shirt tail and vanished into the cinderblock building. I sat down on a nearby bench.

Camille was dead, but she clung to my skin like smoke. She and Peter both had shown me something I could not ignore. I should accept it. I had to accept it. It was the truth. But there was something of the ego that refused to let it in. It was a fear of being diminished. I didn't want to admit that I had fallen for everything Camille stood for. I had. I had imbibed it from birth. The only real question, though, was how long her hold on me would last.

I sat on the bench, listened to the city sounds around me. The slap of water against pylons. The cry of the gulls overhead. The murmur of voices around me. Cars growling and beeping as they made their way up Ocean Drive.

We were both on administrative leave now. There was a chance Peter would lose his job. And Camille finally had her fame…and that let me see a part of what Peter meant. Why had people liked Camille? Why were they forgiving her now? Why did what she put all of us through matter so little? The answer opened before me like a corpse-flower.

It wasn't about Camille. It was about what she let me pretend I don't say. All of us, really. Through her, we could view the history she built with a nostalgic lens, blurred so one can ignore the blood and bones under the honey sweet fantasy. And that's the point. When you bury a body, you don't want to admit it. And we had earthed more than our fair share. Camille, lovely in her dresses with her clean, dead hands, the reenactors with their coats and stars-and-bars. The fake Marilyn Monroe, glaring daggers at Peter. All of it was part of the same disguise for history's shallow grave.

This was an unforgivable sin.

We are all narcissistic to a point. We want to be featured in somebody else's story, to be absolved of the things we do, to be permitted to erase the pain we cause without first making true amends. And we don't want to see the truth in our reflection. These are the animate bones we fear. And like the witch of Coos, it isn't chance we fear them. We know where the bodies are. We're the ones who put them there.

I bore some blame for what happened today. It would be so easy to deny it. I hadn't given Camille the tools, but I was part of what made things like Camille possible. And now that I knew it, inaction was no longer an option.

I couldn't save Peter. I couldn't even save myself. He did that. It was his victory. And nothing I could give him would ever equal what he had just done for me. But I could break the things that gave Camille and those like her power. I could be heartless with memory.

It wasn't much, but it was the best I could do.

Sometimes Corpus Christi is magical. The gazebos every hundred yards or so gleamed like a string of carefully separated pearls. Tourists wandered up and down the beachfront, many of them playing Augmented Reality games on their phones. Seagulls muttered to themselves, complaining in high pitched voices as they wheeled across the sky. There were other, not-human things about too. I spotted members of the local werewolf pack, both shifted and not, walking in a tight huddle around each other's phones. I could hear the Faerie busker up by the Irish Pub playing a saxophone. The kid was only half Fae. He was working his way through a fusion of Irish folk melodies and the Blues. Every few breaths of wind, the otherworldly sound he coaxed out of his instrument drifted my way.

After about ten minutes, Pete returned. No bag.

Our world is an exceptional place, but even the most magical things often have mundane resolutions; that's part of what makes the journey so worthwhile. "Did you flush?" I asked.

"It took a couple times. The death of the last great Southern Belle," He said, then sighed. Dropped his head for a second. The wind picked up, and he heard it too: The saxophone. It made him smile. "I love it when Jimmy starts working the Laughing Gull. Is that La Vie en Rose?"

"Sounds like it," I said.

He listened, eyes closed, head back, wind and sun on his face. Happy Pete. Gee, I'd really missed that guy. "Yeah. He ain't Louis but he ain't bad. I want a beer. Irish pub?"

"Irish pub," I agreed, "After you."

And I stepped back out of Peter's way.

Obviously, the subject matter in this book is sensitive. In the past few years we have elevated our mainstream awareness of issues such as systematic prejudice and racism. Unfortunately, the inequalities themselves have a well established precident. They have florished in our society's silence and willful ignorance, and will continue to grow as long as silence remains.

I did not write about these issues because I have anything new to add. I know my voice in this cause is surpurfluious and unnecessary, and that this book contributes little to no value to the greater issues at hand. Most of it was beyond my experience. However, these things are real. They happen every day, and with increasing malice. And to exclude them from a work of fiction that is based in our world is to say either that these things do not happen, or they are not of sufficient importance to include.

I know I got a lot wrong. I know that I cannot equal the perspective of someone who has actually endured these things. I tried to present these issues with clarity and honesty. I know that it is inevitable that I failed in the task. But inaction can no longer be anyone's option. I would rather fail and be rightfully criticized for failing than stay safe and pretend like everything is fine.

It isn't. And it hasn't been for a very long time.

We need to do better.

Sincerely,
Chelsea Gaither.

Read on for a sample chapter of
STONE'S THROW
the next exciting novel in the
Terrestrial Affairs universe
Avaliable May 2021

Chapter One

The Senator from Texas almost died on Friday.

On Monday, I walked into work juggling the three Cs of Terrestrial Affairs: Coffee, computer and case files. It'd been a busy week. One of our ghost cases had turned into a full-blown non-consensual exorcism, and that always came with the kind of paperwork that made drinking yourself into oblivion a logical coping skill. Consensual exorcisms are relatively easy. You just have to find a good therapist and a spirit-sensitive priest who can come in at the agreed-upon last session and witness the ghost leaving this plane of existence. A non-con usually goes ugly fast. If the entity is the non-consenting party, they tend to punish the host. Doing obnoxious things to family members, pulling the body into painful contortions. Bodily fluids tend to feature prominently. Fortunately, in this case it was the host who was clinging to the ghost. It had been a relative who had been a very skilled painter, and the possession occurred because the ghost had wanted to teach their niece how to paint. Unfortunately for the ghost, the niece figured it would be easier to just get the dead person to paint things for them.

Normally a ghost possession is less of an emergency than, say, a malignant poltergeist or a demon. A ghost is not a complete being. They're fragments and splinters of a true soul, and without regular magical reinforcement they decay rapidly. Too rapidly to do any long-term damage to the host's brain or personality. But the niece was getting regular "recharges" from a neighborhood spirit-worker and was beginning to lose major chunks of her own memory.

And so we had to do the whole song and dance, complete with bell, book and candle. This time the priest was not a rubber stamp, but one with a doctorate and a couple master's degrees in both magical theory and psychology. In the end it took both him and our resident witch, Magdalena, two hours to actually draw the spiritual morass inside this girl into the open and untangle them both piece by piece.

So we had to have a form for that, witnessed by a third sensitive. And then we had to have a form for the psychology work the ghost had needed—accepting that you are merely a fragment of your former self, the psychic version of shattered safety glass, isn't easy—and a form for involuntary committal of the host, who had implied she was a risk to herself and others about nine times during the whole mess. And I had to write up every action taken and try to make it fit under one of the government issued categories so that all of it was billable to the multiple insurance companies and government oversight agencies involved. I'm not afraid of demons these days as much as I am of the Joint Commission. This, on top of my normal case-load, which added about two hours of paperwork per day.

It had taken most of the weekend to catch up.

I almost ran over my partner, Peter Jennings. He was doing the same juggling act, albeit with far more panache. He looked like a Black Ichabod Crane, all long angles and shockingly red hair, but when he moved it was like watching silk pass through a ring. His hair was a few shades darker than Celtic ginger, and a lot of people assumed that he dyed it. He didn't. Those who knew it was natural would then assume that he was some kind of mage—there is a tradition in America and several European countries that a Black man with red hair is a born sorcerer. Pete hates both the assumption and the tradition. One of his public speaking presentations in college had been on how that tradition was mostly in countries that profited from the slave trade. He had a whole PowerPoint on the subject. A couple weeks ago he'd even let me borrow it.

He looked exhausted. He'd finally begun dating again—Peter and I had bonded, in part, over our catastrophic taste in men--this time a guy he met at the local Irish pub. A very, very pretty white boy who reminded me of my ex so profoundly I'd felt compelled to pull Peter aside and recite the narcissist's prayer to him. But I'd still hoped I was wrong. Peter joked a lot about how gay relationships age in dog years, but he'd opened up to me once about how sometimes just the stress of walking into the Water Street Ocean Bar together could implode a relationship. South Texas has gotten better, but it still isn't exactly a powerhouse of LGBT rights. He'd had a great bounce in his step last week. I guess his weekend had gone even worse than mine.

"You need any help getting your half squared away?" I asked, gesturing with my casefiles.

He shook his head, a bit longer than what the casefiles needed. I read this as two things: No, he did not need my help and no, he did not want to talk about his weekend. I complied, and simply paced him as we walked up to our desks.

Terrestrial Affairs Corpus Christi Headquarters sits somewhat near the bayfront, between the new Federal Courthouse—neat, trim, with echoes of a dude ranch cowboy—and the old—a moldering abandoned building. The latter is on the historical registry so it cannot be demolished, but the state of decay—not to mention the unpaid property tax—is so severe that no one has successfully remodeled it. Emergency repairs sit on the building in an increasing patchwork of desperation. It is not, despite many rumors to the contrary, haunted. CCTA would be in poor shape if we allowed ghosts to flourish so close to our headquarters.

The building itself is a boring, nondescript beige. If a post office and a warehouse had a baby, it would be our building. It is surrounded by a near-wall of overgrown, pale pink oleanders. The poisonous bushes make an excellent privacy barrier, as they are harder to kill than most cockroaches and, when permitted, will outgrow whatever they're planted in. Ours had to be chopped back twice a year. We were at the mid-point, where it looked like they'd been untouched from seedling on up. We'd chop them back when it looked like they were about to pull up roots and start consuming people.

I'd noticed a few unusual cars in the parking lot. Our clients run the gamut from dirt poor to very wealthy and lived everywhere from Leopard Street on up to Ocean Drive's big mansions. But what we didn't see a lot of were other government vehicles. The relationship between CCPD and TA is frosty to say the least. They get territorial when we show up, and we see them as barely restrained cowboys. Ergo, we aren't going to get along. Our own vehicles are unmistakably government issue, but they at least come in colors. Red, gray, green, silver. Today, there was a row of black sedans where our morning workshop participants usually parked. But I wasn't sure something was going on until I walked into the building.

There's usually a murmuring that greets you, because TA is almost always busy. One of the bigger jobs that falls under our mandate are vampires. We keep the building open 24/7. A well-fed vampire is just a night owl with odd dietary habits and a need for SPF nine-billion. A hungry one is a risk to everybody in their neighborhood, including themselves. The local blood banks set aside a supply of less-than-ideal donor blood for vampires and we have a small fridge stocked with enough blood to get five to six clients through the night.

We try to run two or three workshops a week during dayshift. How to manage lycanthropy, witchcraft 101—aka basic wards and charms—and Ghosts and Hauntings are our three most popular. Mondays were the wolf-shop, when the local Alpha, Dame Madra would show up with a couple sandwich trays and a case of soda pop. Agents love Mondays. Madra and her wife, Yuki, have great taste in food and We get the leftovers. But this morning her corner was empty. Neither her, her pack, her wife or her kids were present. The lights in that conference room were off.

Nor was anyone cloistered in one of the numerous small alcoves set up with chairs, tissue boxes and a nearby source of water. Meaning either nobody was seeking help today, or we'd been told to turn people away at the door.

I'd only ever seen that happen once. And that had been a very bad day.

I looked up. The second floor is open, loft style, to the entrance atrium. This allows senior agents to have a space apart from the general public—necessary to preserve client confidentiality—while still having an ear out for whatever was going on downstairs. Even the sounds of work—phones ringing, hands typing, printers coughing out pages—was muted. And nearly nobody was talking.

Agents gossip. We like to pretend we don't, and most of us are smart to leave client information out of it, but we will absolutely dissect each other around the coffee machine each and every day. Our current crop of interns had either all dropped out or were on their way to becoming probationary agents, so talking about them had lost some of the usual luster, but our Muslim staff heretic—when you deal in esoteric magic-gone-bad, a good heretic is worth their weight in gold, especially if they practice a different religion than you--Ahmed ben Salid, was struggling through his oldest daughter's rather…Americanized love-life. We also had a new guy in Historical Research who was basically gossip bait himself. He kept to himself and absolutely stank of magic himself. There are only two events that can completely silence the floor: Something happens in the Boss's office, or somebody dies.

"Maybe Lavell finally strangled Arrows with a cat 5 cable," Peter said.

"Maybe." I said. Dominique Lavell was one of the surviving interns. She struck you on introduction as being this fragile little flower, but once the pressure got turned up she was one tough cookie. She also had made it a point to make friends, though it had taken her a bit to open up to being trans. Max Arrows, the other intern, was much less popular. As he and I hadn't really worked together yet, all I could go by was the opinions of others. Magdalena Gonzales avoided him at all costs. Peter had decked him a few months ago over some rather insensitive, not to mention stupid, remarks during a very bad case. In short, we all figured it was just a matter of time before Domi finally throttled the guy and put the rest of us out of our misery.

But that didn't explain the oppressive silence that suddenly filled the building.

The elevator going up to the second floor has to have been some reject from a horror movie. The fluorescent lights not only flicker when the doors close, they change tone from warm to cold when the engine engages. The whole carriage moves with a jittery, sea-sick lurching that makes me white knuckle whatever I am carrying. But when I'm tired, in a hurry, or juggling papers I can't lose it's still better than taking the stairs. It dinged cheerfully as it let us out onto the floor.

Everyone had their heads down, looking intently at the monitor screens.

I glanced at the glass-walled breakroom out of reflex, but the TV wasn't talking about any big disaster. Okay, nothing newsworthy was currently on fire. But what could be so serious that not one of my coworkers was interested in goofing off?

Peter and I were both still on thin ice. A client had died on our watch and we'd been suspended until an investigation had cleared us—and that was the official story that we were sticking to on pain of being fired. I can't be sure what drove Peter to his desk without stopping to ask what new, fresh hell was motivating the office atmosphere, but it was probably the same employment concerns that propelled me towards mine.

Technichally, Agents at TA are paired. However, TA has found that doesn't help the issue of Agent mortality. Partners in a close working relationship are still vulnerable to a folie-a-deux, and that's not good when you're dealing with reality warping clients. A triad is also not beneficial. Sartre's demons might have been inaccurate, but he was right in one department: Hell is other people. A trio naturally causes odd people out, and those odd-outs tend to die. So the working reality of TA is a quartet: Two sets of two. But Peter and I had spent most of the last year as a duo. After last Halloween's fiasco, we were overdue for a new third and fourth member.

So I should not have been surprised to see Max Arrows sitting in the free chair at Peter's cubicle, while IT was setting up his computer. Chagrined, yes, but not surprised.

I looked at Peter. Peter's jaw looked like he was about to pop some teeth. He settled himself, strode to his desk like a man walking into fire, and set his laptop and casefiles down on the smooth, black tabletop. "So. I take it you're my new partner?"

"Probationary," Max said. He didn't look at Peter. "How long does it take to hook wires up to a box?"

The IT tech was Jade Xiao. She was one of those happy smiley people who would look genuinely gleeful at her own funeral. Her smile was undimmed. Her grip on her tools, however, was much tighter than normal. "We have regulations," She said, and pointed at the large box of protective clips that had to go on each wire. These were standard issue spell-circuits. Everybody who deals with protected information has to use them. They're in banks, hospitals, and even supermarkets. If you have to swipe a card, odds are you'll find a few of these clips somewhere in the circuitry. They're something of a failsafe. If they detect unauthorized magic finessing its way up the wires they guard, they shut everything off.

"Yeah, but you could put those on when we're done. I want to get to really work." Max said.

"If you don't have the clips on, you don't access our databanks. Without that, you can't work at all," Jade said. She sounded like a kindergarten teacher lecturing a recalcitrant student.

He sighed and crossed his arms.

Funny. I kept thinking the guy was young. Dominique Lavell, for example, was in her late twenties, and she registered as the oldest intern we had. But she wasn't. Max was pushing forty. I wasn't sure why he read as younger than Domi. Maybe it was his height. The man looked like half a fireplug.

"Hey, Jade," I said. She glanced at me, nodding permission to continue as she continued to clip little magic watch-eyes to USB cables. "What's going on?"

"What do you mean?" She said.

"The last time it was this quiet was when one of our agents got caught with succubi," I said. That agent had survived. His capacity for future erotic encounters hadn't.

She glanced at Max, then sighed as if steeling herself for something unpleasant. "The FBI showed up today. They're still in conference with Director Augustine."

"Shit," Peter said. "Who fucked the dog this week?"

Jade stopped applying clips. "Nobody. They had me in there to install some watchers on a feed directly from Quantico. They're bringing us into an investigation."

I heard a sound from inside our director's office. It was one of the few closed rooms on this floor, and it was not sound proof. You could always hear Director Augustine when she got angry. That sounded like a four-point-oh on the Pissed meter. You really didn't want her to get much past a five.

"They're ticking her off that much?" Peter said.

"I haven't ever heard her scream before," Max agreed.

"I don't think it's the agents. They were keeping mum and looking worried." Jade said, then quickly wrapped up her job on Max's computer. "Whatever's going on, somebody else in another agency screwed it up."

"You gonna set me up with Domi next?" I said, hopefully.

Jade smiled and shook her head. "Rumor says Domi is dating one of your clients. She asked for the occult watch. As for you, Arrows…you're all set." She tapped the computer box and smiled. With teeth. "Have fun."

She turned around and left.

I was about to make a pithy comment about Max's welcome when I saw movement out of the corner of my eye. Director Augustine's office had opened. A tall, Black woman stepped out. She was nearly model slender, and easily the tallest person on the floor. Her skin was the burnished dark of wrought iron, and her brown gaze as it surveyed the floor made one think of hawks, eagles and falcons. She allowed it to rest here and there in the room, as if measuring the abilities of those she found.

And then she saw me and smiled.

My gut plummeted.

"Stone. Jennings. Arrows. My office." She said, with just the lightest hint of Britain in her vowels.

"Nice way of asking," Max grumbled, and fished his coat out of his chair.

Peter and I exchanged another look. "You wanna take bets on how long he's gonna last?" Peter asked.

I said nothing. I knew better than to take a sucker bet.

ABOUT THE AUTHOR

Chelsea Gaither was born in the 80s and grew up catching venomous caterpillars in the live oak scrub around Corpus Christ, TX. They currently live around Dallas with a toddler and lots of books.

This is their least favorite part of the book.

www.ingramcontent.com/pod-product-compliance
Lightning Source LLC
Chambersburg PA
CBHW061432160726
47995CB00003B/862